THE LEADING MAN

A novella by

Noah Khan

eBook ISBN: 979-8-9906821-2-2
Paperback ISBN: 979-8-9906821-3-9

ALSO BY NOAH KHAN

Princes

This story is dedicated to my family. Just like Caleb's family, you always encourage and support me. Thank you for everything! This story is also dedicated to my late grandmother, Perla, aka Mangas. I miss you dearly and love you so much.

CHAPTER 1

Aaron

CELEBRITY TABLOID
Aaron Remington Has Public Meltdown!
September 7th, 2018

This past Friday, paparazzi captured footage of Hollywood actor Aaron Remington having a public meltdown while seemingly intoxicated. Remington, best known for his work in the *Moonlight Galaxy* blockbuster trilogy, was seen yelling at a server at a high-class restaurant in Los Angeles. When Remington noticed paparazzi filming, he attacked them with obscenities and violent threats, even throwing food and drink at them. To make matters worse, Remington also attempted to destroy the paparazzi's camera equipment.

Is this the end for Aaron Remington?

Remington's manager and agent could not be reached for comment.

2023

I took a drag of my cigarette and put the crumpled magazine article down. I was pretty sure I read this same damn article at least once a day. I knew it couldn't be good for me, just like this cigarette. But, hey. It was like looking at a car crash; part of you knows you should look away, but you just can't. There was something horrifically mesmerizing about it.

Is this the end for Aaron Remington?

I couldn't tell you the answer. Although, it seemed like everyone else knew. And the answer was a resounding *yes.* Hollywood had officially canceled Aaron Remington. After all, who would want to work with an asshole like me? I stared at the pictures in the article, of me throwing things at the paparazzi with a crazed expression on my face, looking like a maniac. A surge of shame welled up in me, but I pushed it down. I stood up from the kitchen table, put out my cigarette, and retreated to a room at the end of the hall. I unlocked the door and stepped inside what I called my "Trophy Room." It was like a massive storage room, filled with my literal trophies and awards, most of them for *Moonlight Galaxy*. I looked around the room, at the framed *Moonlight Galaxy* posters hanging on the wall and of my awards: *Best Child Actor in a Motion Picture. Best Leading Child Actor in a Science Fiction Film.* Golden Globes. Emmy's. Even an Academy Award nomination (for which I was snubbed).

You'd think it would all mean something, that it would make me proud. But all I feel is shame. Maybe I should rename this my "Shame Room." I took one of the posters off the wall. Behind it was a little safe. I opened it and tucked in the crumpled magazine article, then put the framed poster back on the wall and sighed.

Is this really what my life has come to? Reminiscing on the past, on my success, and my failures? What a joke.

I was locking up the room again when I heard my phone ring. I frowned. How odd. I never got text messages anymore, let alone phone calls. I took my phone out of my pocket and looked at the Caller I.D.— *Rebecca.* Now I was really confused. My mother barely had time to talk to me, so her calling me was out of the blue. I hovered my finger over the *decline* button but ultimately answered the call. That was a big mistake, I would later find out.

"Hi, Aaron. It's your mother."

"Um…hi?" I wasn't surprised by her tone. It was curt and official, as if she were talking to a client rather than her own son.

"Your father and I are flying in tonight. We have some…things we'd like to discuss with you."

I was silent. My parents want to talk with me *in person*?

I recovered myself. "Um…I'd have to check my schedule, but I'll let you know if—"

My mother cut me off. "Oh, I think we both know that you're free. We'll be flying in and will visit you tonight. Goodbye, Aaron." She hung up.

What the hell?

A wave of uneasiness washed over me. What were they planning?

Whatever it was, it couldn't be good.

Before the sun had fully set, the doorbell rang. I took a deep breath. It was pathetic; I was nervous to see my own parents. I checked my reflection in the mirror and then opened the door. My mother and father stood there like vampires waiting to be invited in. I opened the door a little wider and they finally walked in, looking around the place. My mother wore a black Dolce & Gabbana dress with a matching handbag; my father wore a crisp Dior suit and tie. This was their *casual* wear. In my blue jeans and red flannel, I may as well have been naked. My mother studied me closer, turning her nose upright as though she smelled something foul.

"Hello, Aaron," my mother said in her usual official tone. My father gave me a curt nod. I nodded back at them and then there was silence. My mother and father looked at each other and then looked back at me.

"Aaron…" my father started. He seemed at a loss for words, a first for him.

My mother intervened. "Aaron, you may want to sit down for this."

My eyes narrowed. *Were they serious?* I sighed and went to the living room and sat on the leather couch. My parents followed and stood in front of me. My mother pursed her lips. "Aaron, your father and I think it's time…for you to take on some…responsibility."

I raised an eyebrow. Since when did my parents give a flying shit about my *responsibility*? My father stepped in.

"What your mother is trying to say is that we both think you should learn how to handle finances yourself."

Oh. So this was about money. Of fucking *course*. I should have known. I ran my hands through my dark hair. "So, what?" I asked. "Are you loaning me less money every month?"

My parents were silent for a moment. Then my mom stepped forward. "Actually, your father and I have decided to stop loaning you money *at all*." She stepped back and seemed to have some relief, ripping off the band aid.

Silence.

I stood up in disbelief. "You...you're *cutting me off?*"

My father shook his head. "Don't think of it like that; we're trying to help you learn some responsib—"

"Oh, don't give me that bullshit! Since when did either of you ever care about my *responsibility* or teaching me anything? All you do is call once or twice a year and fling wads of money at me as some sort of compensation!" I paced the room, getting heated. All the words were starting to just...come out, all of the pushed down feelings. "Admit it; you both never cared about me, only about your reputations and seeming like the *perfect* little family. And now you just waltz in here saying you're taking away the only thing you've ever *given* me?" I laughed bitterly. "Well, no. I'm not gonna take that. So, you both can just take your high-and-mighty selves out of *my* house and *fuck off.*"

Alright, maybe I went a bit too far. My parents were silent. When my mother recovered, she cleared her throat. "We've already cut your credit cards and put the lease back in your name. It's done."

My eyes must have been bulging out my head because my father looked at me with pity and said, "Oh, Aaron. You really should have seen this coming."

I really fucking should have.

CHAPTER 2

Caleb

"Vanessa, I want you to know that I'll always be here for you." I cupped her cheek and stroked her face. She looked up at me, tears glistening in her eyes.

"But, what about our parents? You know they'll never accept our relationship!" Vanessa cried.

I smiled reassuringly. "Don't worry. Whatever happens, you'll always have me by your side." I leaned down and softly kissed her, wrapping my arms around her waist. When I gently pulled away, we stared longingly into each other's eyes.

"CUT!" the director, Marcus, shouted. "Alright everyone, break for lunch!" He walked up to us, grinning from ear to ear. "Caleb, Alison, that was an amazing performance. Exactly what I was looking for."

I smiled, feeling happy and proud to hear this. Marcus nodded, and continued, "You both have amazing chemistry. You two have the makings of a Hollywood 'it' couple!"

Alison seemed pleased to hear this, but my happiness was turning into something else. I couldn't place what it was... shame? Guilt? Whatever it was, I brushed it off and grinned back at Marcus.

"Alright guys, have a good lunch," he said and walked over to the camera operator.

I turned to Alison. "Great job! I'll see you in a bit!" I went to walk off set when Alison pulled me back. She flashed a dazzling smile, her teeth bright white. She tossed her blond hair over her shoulder.

"Actually, I was wondering if you wanted to grab lunch somewhere…together?"

I stood still for a moment and was about to say yes when I realized the implications of this invitation. Oh. *Oh.* I looked past Alison and saw my other co-star, Brent, staring from across the set. Butterflies flew in my stomach and my heartbeat quickened. I focused my attention back on Alison.

"Actually…I'm sorry but I-I can't today. Maybe another time?" Alison seemed surprised. Of course she was. After all, she probably wasn't used to being turned down. She nodded slowly.

"Oh, yeah. Sure. Just let me know." Then she walked away, flipping her blond hair again. I looked back at Brent, who was still staring at me, with his hazel eyes and side-swept bangs. He nodded at me, and I knew exactly what that meant.

It was time.

"You're so fucking hot," Brent said as he shoved his tongue into my mouth.

"So are you," I said as I explored his mouth with my tongue. We were making out in his Ferrari F8 Tributo, the windows tinted and a sun shield covering the dashboard. It wasn't the most comfortable place for a hook-up session, but I didn't care at this point. I needed to have *some* sort of relief. And Brent was super-hot. With his hazel eyes, a crinkly smile, and dimples, there was nothing unattractive about him. He clumsily fumbled for my zipper and pulled down my briefs, my hard cock shooting out. Brent grinned and began sucking me off, deepthroating me almost immediately. I groaned and leaned my head back, with my hand resting on his soft, brown hair as he bobbed up and down. Eventually, I felt the climax coming in from my toes, extending outward to my thighs.

"I-I'm close," I whispered, shaking. Brent bobbed his head up and down faster, stroking me at the same time and I cried out, spilling my seed. Brent swallowed my cum professionally, and I took deep breaths, recovering myself. Brent looked up at me, his mouth red and wet.

"How was that?" he asked, his eyes crinkling. I nodded slowly.

"You were amazing, as usual." Brent leaned back into his seat, wiping his mouth with a napkin. He took a deep breath and looked at me, now all business.

"Alright, you know the drill. I'll leave and you wait fifteen minutes before following." I opened my mouth to reassure him, but he was already turning to leave. Before he left, he stared at me intensely. "And remember. Don't tell *anyone* about this. If anyone finds out, it will ruin *both* of our careers." And then he slammed the car door shut.

I sat there in silence, with that familiar feeling welling up inside me. I couldn't tell if it was shame or anger, but I guess it didn't matter. I knew from the beginning that these hook-up sessions would have to remain a secret, just like my own secret I had to keep from the world. Before I knew it, tears were welling in my eyes. *What the fuck? Was I that pathetic?* I had told myself it would have to be this way if I wanted a successful career in this business. I couldn't afford to lose it now, not with my reputation as the "leading man." I looked around the dark car, wondering if it would always be this way. Sneaking around, lying. I dried my eyes. *Get ahold of yourself. You should be grateful. Other people would kill to have the life you have.*

Has it been fifteen minutes yet?

"How was your shoot?" Lucy asked while slurping from her bowl of ramen. I took a stab at my teriyaki chicken and peered at her over my dark-rimmed sunglasses.

"Oh, it was good. The director seems to think I'm doing a great job."

Lucy smirked. "Of course he does; you're Caleb Robinson after all!" She whispered my name since we were in public—which was why I was also wearing a baseball cap and sunglasses.

Lucy took a sip from her Coke and said, "I still can't believe I'm friends with *the* Caleb Robinson." She shook her head in disbelief. I rolled my eyes, a smile creeping on my lips.

"Oh, please. You've known me since I was, like, ten."

Lucy shrugged. "Yeah, but how was I supposed to know you'd become this big-shot Hollywood actor?"

I gave her a look. "I'm still the same person…just now everyone knows who I am."

Lucy tilted her head. "Yeah, so not a big deal," she said with sarcasm in her tone. I just shrugged modestly. Lucy leaned back in her chair. "Still, I'm happy for you. It was always your big dream to become an actor." She gulped the last of her ramen, some of her long brown hair falling over her shoulder. I looked down at my teriyaki bowl, suddenly not feeling that hungry anymore.

Lucy leaned in closer, with a knowing look. "Something's bothering you." I looked away; of course she could tell. She knew me like the back of her hand, after all.

"It's just…keeping this…secret…it's harder than I thought it would be." Lucy was silent, sympathy in her eyes. I continued. "It's like I'm acting all the time; only it's not fun, it's sad and lonely."

She sighed and wiped her mouth with a napkin. "Does it *have* to be a secret? There are plenty of openly gay actors out there." I knew that, of course I did. I knew that, especially in this day and age, you were encouraged to come out and be yourself in this industry.

"My career is only just taking off. Not only that, but most of my roles have been as the 'straight leading man.'" I looked up into the sky. "If I were to come out, that's all people would see me as. That one *gay* actor. I don't know if I could handle that." It was weird; I'd always been out and proud about my sexuality, never was ashamed of it. Now it seems like I've taken five steps backwards ever since my newfound success.

Lucy nodded. "Well. Maybe one day, you won't have to hide it anymore."

I smiled weakly. Yeah, maybe one day.

CHAPTER 3

Aaron

I was truly and most definitely fucked. This realization came right after my parents' visit, while I drank from a bottle of vodka at two in the morning. The TV was on, playing a black-and-white rerun of some old sitcom. After everything I did for them, going into show business and becoming a star like they wanted. As if I were a trophy and nothing more. I shook my head and took another swig from the bottle. *Motherfuckers.*

Of course, it wasn't completely their fault. I was a moron too. After all, you're probably thinking: Well, Aaron, don't you have millions of dollars from *Moonlight Galaxy?* I did…at one time. Before the drinking, and the partying, and the drugs. I was *drowning* in dollar bills. Just another thing Aaron Remington fucked up. I still had some money left, enough to keep me afloat while I figured my shit out. I stared at the black-and-white screen, my vision blurring. I sniffed and picked up my cell phone. *Zero missed calls.* As usual. I thought for a moment…should I call my sister? No, that was a bad idea. We haven't talked in ages, and I knew she despised me anyway. But I was drinking, and I wasn't in a sensible state-of-mind. My finger hovered over Megan's number for a moment before I thought, *fuck it*, and tapped her name. A couple of rings went by before I heard her say:

"Aaron, what the fuck?! It's two in the fucking morning!"

"I know…I just needed to talk to someone."

"Well, it better be a fucking emergency for calling this late. And why're you calling me? Call your fucking *girlfriend* or something." I hesitated; this was obviously a mistake. But I continued.

"Have you talked to Mom and Dad recently?"

A pause on the other end. "Why are you asking?"

I could hear the disdain in her voice. "Well…have they said anything about me recently?"

Megan sighed on the other end. "If this is about them cutting you off, just know I think you absolutely deserve it."

"You…you *know* about that?" I asked, bewildered.

Megan laughed, but it wasn't a kind laugh. "Know about it? I'm the one who *suggested* it." My blood froze and my heartbeat quickened. Anger pulsed through my veins.

"Megan, what the *fuck*? Why would you do that?" I yelled.

Megan didn't waste any time. "Alright, Aaron. You want to do this now? Let's do this. First off, you made millions of dollars on those shitty sci-fi movies, and you fucking *wasted* all of it on drugs and alcohol. Then, you have this disgusting attitude where you think you're above everyone else. After your fucking meltdown, you tarnished not only your reputation but our *entire* family name! You're never there when we need you and you're bleeding everyone dry. Why do you think I don't call you anymore? Because you're a selfish *asshole*, that's why."

I was stunned. I opened my mouth to respond then closed it, like a fish in a bowl. The worst part of it all was I couldn't even deny those things or say she was wrong. I stared at the Caller I.D. for a moment before saying, "Wow. You really thought *Moonlight Galaxy* was shitty?"

"Oh fuck off, Aaron." Then she hung up.

Well, that went well. I took another long swig of my vodka before crashing down on the couch. I stared at the old sitcom playing, wishing for a moment I could live in one where everything gets solved by the end of the episode. Little by little, my eyes felt heavier and heavier before I drifted off into nothingness...

"Damn. That fucking *sucks,*" Tracy said as she stirred her mojito.

It did fucking suck. It was the next day and I was out with my girlfriend, Tracy Aberdale, who also happened to be a famous model and actress. Alright, she wasn't actually my girlfriend; the truth, Tracy had a girlfriend but obviously didn't want her fans to know that. She was using me as a beard; after all, we were both hot. We looked like a great couple. Not only that, but I liked Tracy a lot and she was pretty much my only friend, so I didn't mind helping. I knew all too well what it's like to hide secrets. I took a drink of my Mimosa and nodded in agreement.

"So what are you gonna do?" she asked.

I sighed in frustration. "I don't fucking know. Find a job? No one is gonna hire me in this business so maybe I'll...I don't know...buss tables or something? Tracy grimaced and I had to agree—it was pathetic. Going from stardom to bussing tables was a serious downgrade.

"I cannot see you *bussing* tables," Tracy said, laughing at the thought. I narrowed my eyes but truthfully, I couldn't either.

"I also found out it was my sister who came up with the whole 'cutting me off' plan."

Tracy gaped at this news. "No kidding...what a great sister." I went silent for a moment. I had thought the same, but after her little speech last night, I couldn't entirely blame her.

"The truth is…I think she may be right. I mean, look at me. I was handed success and money on a silver platter, and I blew it to smithereens. I ruined our family's reputation and I had to go to *fucking* rehab." I laughed bitterly. "I'm a complete fucking mess."

Tracy looked at me with sympathy. "Aaron…yes, you may be a complete mess. Have you made some serious mistakes? Yeah. Have you treated people badly in the past? Yeah. But tell me this: who fucking *hasn't?* Tracy leaned back in her chair. "Everyone makes mistakes. I've made many of my own, trust me. It doesn't mean you can't pull yourself out of it, though."

I didn't know what to say to this. I looked down, contemplating her little pep-talk. I knew she was right; everyone makes mistakes and has regrets.

But most people aren't Aaron Remington. And most people don't have a public meltdown, either. I didn't think it was possible to come back from this. Not this time.

CHAPTER 4

Caleb

After my shoot, I was exhausted. We'd been filming for several days, and I was ready for it to be done. Not that I didn't enjoy filming; I just was ready to move on to my next project. Plus, I still needed to discuss with my agent and manager what exactly it *was*. I assumed it would be another romance, which was fine. I'm good at those roles and people seem to enjoy it.

It was getting late in the day and all I wanted to do was crash at my apartment, but my parents were hosting a family get-together, and I knew I couldn't miss it. So, I endured the hour-and-a-half drive to Orange County. I pulled up to the familiar house, with its white picket fence and brick-lined roof. I rang the doorbell and could already hear booming voices from inside. The door opened and there was my mother, with her blond hair and a pretty yellow dress that I was pretty sure was from Target. She grinned from ear to ear when she saw me and pulled me in for a big hug. Then she turned her head to the dining room.

"Hey, everybody!" she yelled. "The rising star has decided to make an appearance!" There were cheers and yelps in response.

"Come in; we're playing one of your movies on the TV!" my mom shouted excitedly.

I groaned; *of course* she was playing one of my movies. I feigned annoyance, but in truth it felt good to know my parents were proud of me. After all, I wouldn't be where I was today without their encouragement. Next to greet me was our Chihuahua, Mittens, who leapt from the couch and begged me to rub her tummy.

"Hi sweetie," I said as I scratched her stomach. I walked into the dining room and saw everyone was about to start dinner. It was an understatement to say I had a big family. My younger sister, Sofia, stood up and greeted me with a hug.

"Hiya, playboy."

I swatted her arm playfully. "I told you not to call me that!"

She shrugged. "I liked your newest movie. Very suave performance."

I rolled my eyes. I should have expected this. My siblings always liked to make fun of me for my romance movies. My older brother, Wes, stood up and gave me a hug as well.

"What's up, bro? Saw your latest movie. That actress in it was *hot*." He grinned, shaking his head. "*Of course* my little gay brother gets all the hot babes in Hollywood instead of me."

I punched him on the arm and grinned back. I knew the little quips were their way of showing support. I hugged my grandmother and my cousins, as well as my aunt and uncle who congratulated me on my success. Finally there was my dad. He rose up from his chair and towered above me. He walked over and embraced me with a big hug.

"How's my middle child doing? You doing alright in that overpopulated city?"

I nodded. "Yes, dad, everything is great!" I didn't mention how my secret was taking a toll on me; I didn't want to dampen the mood. I sat down to eat, the air smelling delicious. I missed my mom's homemade cooking. I was such a baby, getting homesick so easily. I grabbed a piece of fried chicken and poured myself some soda.

"So, how is everybody doing?" I asked. My mother peered into the oven to check on dessert and then sat down with us.

"Oh, we're all doing fine! It's the same old-same old in this house; although it has been feeling a bit empty since you and Wes moved out."

"Oh, am I not enough?" Sofia joked. My mom pursed her lips and rolled her eyes.

"Oh, you're *more* than enough." We all laughed. "I just meant that, it's nowhere near as loud as it used to be."

I nodded. When Wes and I lived there, there was always commotion and chaos. Now it was just my parents and Sofia. And soon, she'd be off to college. Then my parents would be by themselves. The thought made me a bit sad, but I brushed it off and took a biscuit. We were all chatting about different things, catching up, when Sofia lightly kicked me under the table.

"What's up?" I asked.

She took a bite of macaroni and cheese before saying, "There's some rumors about you in the media."

My heartbeat quickened and my cheeks went hot. "R-rumors?"

She shook her head. "Don't worry, not about that. I've just been reading your comments and stuff when I'm bored."

Relief surged through my body, and I nodded. "Oh, ok. I try not to look at those. But I am a bit curious. What do people say?"

Sofia looked at her phone and then gave it to me. I looked at the screen; it was a news article—about me:

Is Caleb Robinson just a passing fad?

It seems like the name Caleb Robinson has been on everybody's minds lately. The twenty-three year old actor has quickly made a name for himself with films such as *The Bleeding Rose*, *The Honeymoon*, and *Love Eternity*, to name a few. Although these films and others have launched Robinson to stardom, fans can't help but wonder: will Robinson ever branch out? It seems like all Robinson does are typical romance films. Usually, the characters he plays are of the same formula; good-looking, sweet, and romantic. If Robinson continues like this, it's possible his name might just be a passing fad in the entertainment industry.

I didn't bother reading the rest. I pushed the phone back to Sofia. I knew I shouldn't care what some tabloid thought; I had already proven myself. But I couldn't help but wonder if the article was right. *Was I already typecast as the leading man?* Were romance movies the only thing I'd get cast in? Worry filled my body. Maybe I should talk to my agent about this. Sofia looked at me.

"I didn't mean to worry you. I just thought you should know what some people are saying. Obviously, these people are just stupid and don't know anything." I nodded back, but I wasn't so sure.

Was there a way to prove that article wrong?

When it was time for me to head back to L.A., everyone gave me a big hug and wished me luck. I pet Mittens and kissed her forehead. As I went to leave, my parents followed me outside. I hugged them one last time before getting in my car.

"Are you sure nothing is bothering you?" my mom asked. I smiled at her reassuringly.

"Don't worry, guys. I got this!" I gave a thumbs-up. They nodded and waved goodbye as I pulled out of the driveway. On the way back, my thoughts kept going back to that stupid article. *Was* I just a passing fad? I sure hoped not. Becoming an actor had always been my dream, and I didn't want anything to jeopardize that. As I neared my apartment, I saw that I had a text come in. *From Brent.* My heart sped up and I clicked on the text.

Wanna come over tonight?

I hesitated; should I come over? I thought for a moment before replying, *yes*.

Maybe some fun would take my mind off things.

"That was amazing," Brent said as we both lay on his bed, breathing heavily. I nodded in agreement, my ass throbbing. Brent and I had spent hours fucking this way and that. I could feel his cum dripping down my stomach where he'd shot his load. I looked at Brent who had his eyes closed with his arms behind his head, recovering from his climax. If only this could be something real. Something like a real relationship. But I knew better; that was not a possibility.

Brent opened his eyes and looked at me. "What're you still doing here?" he asked. I don't think he meant it in a mean way; just that we had done the deed and... now what? Oh. *Oh.* He wants me to leave. Right. I sat up and began getting dressed. As I finished Brent looked at me with that same serious expression.

"Remember, exit from the back and make *sure* no one sees you." I smiled faintly and nodded, as if this were completely fine. I began making my way out when I stopped and turned.

"Brent..." I started. He raised an eyebrow, waiting for me to go on. What did I even want to say? Will you be my boyfriend? Will you stop treating me like a dirty secret? I shook my head. "Just...goodnight," I finished. Brent just nodded back, and I left his apartment, exiting from the back to the parking lot. I got into my car and just sat there, basking in the silence and chirping crickets.

Tears trickled down my face. This was supposed to make me feel *better*.

So why did I feel even worse?

CHAPTER 5

Aaron

I was spending my Friday night watching an old *Moonlight Galaxy* movie on DVD. With a gin and tonic. That's how low I've gotten. What I should have been doing was searching for a job. I needed one desperately after my family decided to fuck me over. I watched my younger self on screen; I was at the part where my character said goodbye to his mom before heading off to fight an intergalactic space war. Fun stuff. I pulled out my laptop and went to Google. The cursor blinked at me mockingly.

What kind of job was I even supposed to get? Besides acting and modeling, I didn't have qualifications for much else. It's not like I went to college; after all, who needs college when you're starring in a multi-billion-dollar franchise? At least, that's what I thought at the time. Now it came back to bite me in the ass. I tried searching for *jobs near me*, but I was qualified for about zero of the jobs that came up. I couldn't cook. I had no sales or retail experience. No experience answering phones. Who the fuck wants that? I sighed angrily and shut my laptop. I looked back at me on the screen. If only I could talk to my younger self now, tell him not to fuck things up so badly.

I turned the TV off. There was no use in living in the past. I needed to figure my shit out *now*. It's not like I had anyone to help me, either. My parents sure as hell weren't gonna help and neither would my sister. I only had one friend. Everyone else seems to hate me. For good reason, too. I was about to open my laptop again, praying for an answer, when my phone rang. I didn't believe in a higher power, but maybe God or something was listening to me.

It was my agent. Or rather, my *old* agent. After my reputation went sour, I was barely cast in anything. My agent tried here and there to get me parts, but it never went too well. Who wants to work with a psycho? I know I wouldn't. I stared at the Caller I.D., hovering my finger over the answer button and finally answered the call.

"…Hello?"

"Hello, Aaron. This is Ryan, your agent. Remember me?"

"Um…yes?"

"That's the warm welcome I get? Jeez, I figured you'd be more excited to hear from me."

I stood up. "No, I am... I mean, I'm a little confused. We haven't spoken in months."

Ryan laughed on the other end. "Yeah, it's hard to get someone acting roles when they act like an asshole, y'know?"

I should have seen that one coming. "So, what? You're calling me just to remind me that I'm an asshole?" I asked incredulously.

"No, no. I'm sure you already know that. I'm calling because I have a job opportunity for you, if you're interested."

Now *this* was surprising. "What kind of job opportunity?" I inquired.

"Meet me tomorrow at my office at three. I'll explain it to you then."

Then he hung up. I stared at my phone in shock.

Maybe there really was a higher power after all.

"Absolutely not." I pushed the script back to Ryan. He narrowed his eyes in disbelief.

"What do you mean? You're seriously turning it down?"

I stared at him and scoffed. "Aaron Remington *doesn't do* romance movies. Let alone *gay* romance movies." I crossed my arms. Actually, I was bi, but he didn't need to know that.

My old agent stood up, obviously not having it. "Aaron, this is your only chance at returning to the industry. I had to beg, *beg*, the director to let you have this role. This could be your big comeback to Hollywood!" He threw up his hands in frustration.

I leaned back into my chair. "Why are you pushing me so hard for this movie?" I asked.

Ryan sighed and sat back down. "Because you were one of the few clients I had with *real* talent. Raw talent. I want to bring that out in you again. And I know it's a romance film, but this is your only shot at showing the public that you're not just some asshole who flips on waiters and threatens the paparazzi."

I looked down, not wanting to remember that. Ryan looked at me intensely. "Can you *really* afford to say no to this movie?" he asked. The truth was, I couldn't afford to say no. I *needed* money after all. As if reading my thoughts, Ryan said "And, this movie pays the *big bucks*. It's expected to be a big blockbuster hit, a first of its kind. You know, people are wanting diversity and all that stuff these days." I sighed. Could this be the answer I've been looking for? I looked up.

"How much are we talking?"

Ryan smiled. "Now, that's what I like to hear."

CHAPTER 6

Caleb

"And that's a wrap, everybody!" Everyone cheered at this proclamation, including me. The filming for my latest movie was officially done. Alison gave me a hug and Brent came and coolly nodded at me, shaking my hand. Sparks flew through me as our hands touched.

Alison looked at me and said, "Wanna join me for some celebratory drinks at my place?" I opened my mouth to decline, but she looked so hopeful that I couldn't help but smile.

"Sure, that sounds like fun." She seemed pleased at this, and we left the set together, with Brent staring after us. A part of me thought, *good. Let him be jealous.* Alison gave me the directions to her address, and I followed her in my own car. As we pulled up to her house, I couldn't help but gape. Her house was in a gated community, and it was *huge.* I really shouldn't have been surprised; after all, Alison was a very successful actress and model. I pulled up to the driveway, and got out of my car, marveling at the bushes shaped like different animals and the fountain spurting clear blue water. Alison got out of her car and noticed my amazement.

"Do you like it?" she asked, grinning.

"It's beautiful," I replied earnestly. I followed her into the house and the inside was even more stunning, with a big spiral staircase and chandeliers hanging from the ceiling. I followed Alison into the kitchen where she was making us some alcoholic drinks. She handed me a glass.

"Thank you," I said. We both went to sit on the outside deck, where there was a massive heart-shaped pool and jacuzzi. There was a bit of awkward silence as we sipped our drinks. Alison looked at me and spoke up.

"So, how did you like shooting our movie?" I nodded.

"It was fun! I really liked working with you and the rest of the cast." I looked around, realizing something. "We should have invited all the cast," I said. I had a pretty good feeling why Alison only invited me.

She smiled shyly and twirled her hair. "I wanted to spend some time alone with you."

I looked down, feeling guilty. "Actually, I…" I started. It probably wasn't a smart idea to tell her. Alison was nice, but I didn't know how well she could keep a secret. Despite this, my secret was rising up inside of me, desperate to get out. Maybe it wouldn't hurt to tell *one* person. Alison looked at me expectantly with her big blue eyes, waiting for me to go on. I fiddled with my glass.

"Listen, I don't want to lead you on or hurt your feelings. I do really like you. But as a friend." I could see the disappointment on Alison's face despite her trying to hide it.

"Is there someone else?" she asked.

I sighed and looked up into the clear, blue sky. "I'm not sure anymore. But…if I told you something, would you promise to keep it a secret?" Alison nodded. "The truth is…I'm gay." I released my breath and looked at Alison. Who, to my surprise, looked *relieved*. She laughed and set her glass down.

"Of course. That makes so much sense. And here I thought you didn't find me attractive enough or something."

I quickly shook my head. "No, you're stunning, trust me. I just…haven't really told anyone in the business."

Alison went quiet. "Oh, I see. You're afraid, huh?"

I nodded. "A little," I admitted.

Alison took a sip from her drink. "Well, don't worry. Your secret is safe with me. I have *tons* of gay guy friends. Now we can talk about boys!"

I laughed at this. "Thank you, Alison. I appreciate it." We talked and drank some more before I decided it was time for me to head out. I felt a little less weight on my shoulders and felt lighter after coming out to Alison. It felt good to have told *one* person in this business. I said goodbye to Alison and drove away, feeling a little better and more hopeful. Alison had no problem with it; maybe the rest of the world would be the same. As I got near my apartment, I received a phone call from my agent.

"Hey, Caleb. You got a minute to come to the office? I have some things I'd like to discuss with you, if you're free." I felt anxiety run through me. Uh oh.

"Uh…Did I do something wrong?" I heard my agent laugh on the other end.

"No, no, no. You did nothing wrong. I just wanted to talk about your next movie is all."

Relief flooded through me. "Ah, alright. I'll be there as soon as I can!"

My heart froze and I felt sick. I stared at the script in my hands. Was this a joke? Did my agent *know* my secret?

My agent looked at my expression and tilted her head. "Come on; I didn't pick you for a homophobe."

My eyes widened. "I-it's-I'm not-," I stuttered. I took a breath and collected myself. "I'm not homophobic," I finally said.

"Then, what's the problem?" my agent asked.

I stared again at the script in my hands. "It's just…I'm known as the leading man. The *straight* leading man."

My agent nodded in agreement. "And there's our issue." I stared at her, confused.

"Oh, don't tell me you haven't read those articles? The ones that are criticizing you for not branching out and being more diverse in your roles?"

Ah, of course. *Of course* my agent knew about those articles. It was her job, after all.

I tapped on the script. "And you think *this* will fix that?"

My agent shrugged. "Well, why not? It's certainly different than anything else you've done. You've only done straight romance movies. This character is also different; he's more soft-spoken and angsty then the typical charming, confident man you play." My agent stood up. "I'm just saying it would be a good career move. Not only would it show your diversity, but it would also show how you're an ally to the gay community as well."

I paused, not knowing what to say. *What about my secret? Would this give it away?*

My agent put her hands on her desk. "Look, you totally don't have to do it if you're uncomfortable. But I do think it would be good for your career."

I set the script down. "Alright. I'll do it." I hoped I wasn't making a mistake.

CHAPTER 7

Aaron

"So, who exactly is directing this movie?" I asked as I took a bite of my chicken salad. I was having lunch with my agent, going over the details of this new movie. A gay romance movie that I somehow was desperate enough to do. I looked at my agent over my sunglasses; just because I wasn't exactly in the limelight anymore didn't mean there weren't still crazed *Moonlight Galaxy* fans who would do anything to have a picture with me. Therefore, I had to be in disguise while out in public.

My agent looked down at his papers. "Melinda Thompson." I almost choked on a piece of chicken. Melinda Thompson was one of the most successful directors of the decade. He nodded. "Yeah. So you better not fuck this up." I took a sip of my passionfruit martini. Noted. My agent took out a schedule and handed me a copy.

"Alright, filming is gonna commence in two weeks and the location will primarily be in L.A., so no need for international travel thankfully."

I gaped at him and slammed my drink down. "Two weeks?!" I exclaimed. My agent peered over at me from his schedule.

"Aaron, you're lucky you're even *getting* two weeks. Most projects start filming right away, or have you forgotten?" I went silent. It *had* been a minute since my last movie. Plus, I had memorized dozens of lines for *Moonlight Galaxy* in short amounts of times. This should be no different, right?

"And who exactly is playing my love interest? It better not be someone ugly," I scoffed. I was joking, of course. Okay, half-joking.

My agent rolled his eyes. "Oh, he's not ugly, trust me. In fact, he was named the *hottest male celebrity of this year*." Ryan looked at me expectantly. I shrugged. I didn't exactly keep up with stuff like that.

Ryan sighed in frustration. "It's Caleb Robinson, you dimwit."

My eyes almost bulged out my head. "*Caleb Robinson?* You mean, that chump who only stars in those cheesy Hallmark movies? Who looks like he couldn't hurt a fly? *That* Caleb Robinson?" I shook my head in disbelief. *Great.* Ryan was gaping at me, then closed his mouth.

"And this is why no one wants to hire you," he stated matter-of-factly. I narrowed my eyes at him but didn't say anything. My agent continued lecturing me. "You should be *grateful* to be starring alongside Caleb Robinson. Combined with his star power and your anticipated comeback, this will generate a lot of buzz for this movie." I suppose he wasn't completely wrong. Still, Caleb Robinson. He was hot, sure, but also seemed as bland as sawdust. Not only that, but he had this "good golden boy" reputation that really rubbed me the wrong way. Oh, well. All I had to do was get through the filming process and then I'd never have to see him again.

It should be easy as cake, right?

"I still don't see what you're complaining about," Tracy said while sipping her cocktail. I had invited Tracy over for some drinks and was catching her up on my dilemma. "Caleb Robinson is the hottest actor in this business right now, and you'll be getting paid while fixing your reputation. Isn't it a win-win situation?" she asked.

I sighed, sipping my own cocktail. "I guess you're right. I just never thought I'd do a romance film, let alone a romance film with goody-two-shoes Caleb Robinson." I was still in disbelief over the whole thing. Tracy laughed, throwing her head back.

"You haven't even met the guy; at least give him a chance. He can't be *that* bad." I narrowed my eyes. I wasn't so sure about that. Tracy held out her hand. "Can I see the script?" she asked. I dug out the script from my bag and handed it to her.

She studied it for a moment, then smiled. "*The Leading Man*. Oh, this looks cute."

I scoffed. "Yeah, if you're into cheesy rom-coms."

Tracy gave me a look. "Oh, come on. As a bisexual man, you should be happy to do this movie!"

I snatched the script back. "Just because I happen to also like men, doesn't mean you'll catch me waving a rainbow flag at a pride parade."

Tracy just shook her head. "Oh, Aaron. You need to be more confident about who you are!"

I took a swig from my cocktail. "Oh, I'm plenty confident. I'm super-hot and I'm pretty much a pop culture icon."

Tracy sighed. "Maybe I spoke too soon."

I set my drink down and clicked on the T.V. "You know what, let's watch a Caleb Robinson movie and take a swig every time there's a cringe-worthy moment. I'm sure we'll be plastered by the end of it."

Tracy swatted my arm. "Aaron, that's mean." I ignored her and started playing one of Caleb's films called *The Bleeding Rose*. Ugh, even the *title* is cringe. But, as I was watching, I couldn't help but notice certain things.

Like, how Caleb's hair was a very light blond color, and how his eyes were crystal clear blue. Not only that, but this guy was actually a pretty good actor. I continued watching the movie, when I felt Tracy's eyes on me. She was smiling.

"What?" I asked.

"You're *invested* in the movie!"

I gaped, furious at this statement. I shut the T.V. off and stood up. "No, I'm not! I was *invested* by how *bad* it was!"

Tracy shook her head and stood up too. "Whatever you say." Tracy hugged me goodbye and I stood there in the silence. I couldn't help but think about Caleb Robinson, with his sandy colored hair and sea blue eyes. I could see now why he was voted hottest man of the year. I shook this off; *no*. He may be hot but he was still your typical golden boy. He would probably just be a passing fad anyway. The poor kids probably quaking in his boots, having to do a project with an icon like me. I picked up the script for *The Leading Man* and contemplated. Two weeks until filming. That should be enough time to prepare, right?

CHAPTER 8

Caleb

My jaw dropped. "*Aaron Remington?*"

My agent nodded reluctantly. I was at a loss for words. "You mean…the guy who starred in the *Moonlight Galaxy* movies? The guy who had a public meltdown and threatened the paparazzi and flipped out on a waiter? The guy who's an alcoholic and went to rehab? *That* Aaron Remington?"

My agent sighed and sat down at her desk. "Yes, Caleb, that's the one. He'll be playing your love interest. I'm just as flabbergasted as you are."

I shook my head in disbelief. "I haven't heard about him in years…wasn't he canceled by the media?"

My agent shrugged and said, "Apparently. But this film is supposed to act as his 'big comeback' to Hollywood."

I crinkled my eyes in confusion. *Big comeback?* I leaned back in my chair. "I can't believe this. I have to work with this...*psychopath*? And pretend that I'm in love with him too?"

My agent looked at me with sympathy. "I know it's not what you were expecting. But his comeback should help with the movie's success and generate a lot of buzz for the movie. I've heard that Aaron is also on probation; meaning, any violent actions or threats and he will be fired immediately. So, you don't need to worry about that."

I sighed. The only things I knew about Aaron Remington, besides his *Moonlight Galaxy* fame, were only *bad* things. I've heard he's difficult to work with, a pretentious snob, and generally an unpleasant person all around. I knew he came from a wealthy family; his mom's some big-shot author and his dad's some kind of entrepreneur. He was probably handed his career on a silver platter. The thought of this made me angry, considering all the hard work I had to do to get where I was today. *I* didn't have any convenient connections. I realized my agent was expecting an answer from me.

I looked up and slowly nodded. "Alright. I'll...I'll try and make it work." My agent seemed relieved.

"Perfect. Here's a copy of the shooting schedule. You'll start filming in two weeks." I nodded solemnly. Damn. What have I gotten myself into?

"Shut up. Shut *up*." Lucy slammed her hands on the kitchen table of my apartment. "You're gonna be starring in a movie with *the* Aaron Remington?!"

I nodded. "Unfortunately," I replied. Lucy shook her head in disbelief. "My parents are gonna *flip out.* They love the shit out of *Moonlight Galaxy.*"

I gave Lucy a look. "That's not the point." Lucy quickly put on a serious expression. "Oh, right. Your dilemma. Right." Lucy thought about this for a moment. "Well, first off, I don't think this will out your secret. I mean, straight actors play gay all the time, and no one blinks an eye." She paused. "And, yeah, Aaron does seem like an... *interesting* person. But your agent said he would be fired if he did anything violent or weird, right?"

I nodded. "Yeah, that's what she said. But I don't know...I've heard bad things about Remington. That he's spoiled, has a big ego, and is hard to work with."

Lucy sighed. "I get that. But we *all* have to work with people we don't like sometimes. Bad co-workers are just a part of the trade, no matter what industry you're in." She *did* have a point there. Lucy went on. "Just remember what your agent said. This will be a good career move and it'll prove all those tabloids wrong."

I tapped the table with my fingers. "Yeah, you're right. I guess I'll just do the best I can."

Lucy nodded. "Caleb, you're an amazing actor. Aaron is *lucky* to get to work with you. Just do what you normally do, and I'm sure everything will turn out fine." Lucy was right, I thought. I'll just prepare for my role like I normally do, memorize my lines, and hit my mark. If Aaron does the same, then filming will go smoothly. I mean, it can't be *that* bad, right?

CHAPTER 9

Aaron

So, it turns out that time really does fly. Before I knew it, two weeks had passed, and it was the first day of filming. I was fucking *nervous*. And the call time was early as fuck. Five in the fucking morning. This was my first shoot in forever, and I was not exactly feeling prepared. I mean, yeah, I read the script. Overall, it was good, I guess, for a romance movie. I tried to memorize my lines, but fuck, I had a lot of them. I hadn't done this in *years*. I'd assumed it would come naturally back to me, but I guess I was wrong. Not much I could do about it at this point. I took a swig from my flask, just for some liquid courage. I made sure I had my script with me and headed over to the filming location.

I pulled up to the West Hollowood studio, where I was immediately escorted onto set by security. The set was bustling with people working their asses off, people who I assumed were the film crew. I saw the director, Melinda, chatting with her assistant. I felt dumb and useless, just standing there. Eventually, Melinda caught my eye and made her way over to me. *Uh oh.* She was a short woman, with light brown hair and rimmed glasses.

"So," Melinda said, eyeing me up and down. "You're the famous Aaron Remington. You do realize I didn't want you cast in this project, right?" I didn't know what to say to this, but Melinda didn't bother waiting for my response. "I've heard not so great things about you. However, Tracy is a good friend of mine, so I decided to do her a favor." I blinked in confusion. *Tracy?* Melinda looked at me, expectantly. "You know...Tracy Aberdale. As in, you*r girlfriend*, Tracy?" I nodded as if I knew what she was talking about. Of course. Fucking *Tracy* set this all up. I would have to remember to yell at her later. Melinda just shook her head. "Anyway, I'm just here to warn you. Any violent outbursts or threats, and you're done. As in, you're fired and there are no second chances. Do we understand?"

I was taken aback. "Um...yes, ma'am."

Melinda nodded. "Good. Your man is over there, studying his script. Maybe you should go introduce yourself."

I turned my head and saw none other than Caleb Robinson. He was sitting on his chair with his script in hand, making notes and intensely reading. I swallowed. Seeing him on screen didn't do him justice. His wavy blond hair was even lighter in person, and I could notice some freckles on his cheeks. I slowly made my way over to him. When he looked up, our eyes met. His blue eyes staring into mine. Caleb stood up and made his way over to me. He held out his hand.

"Hi, nice to meet you. I'm Caleb. Caleb Robinson." My heart leapt to my throat. So. This was Caleb Robinson. I could see now why he was Hollywood's leading man. I stared at his hand and finally shook it.

"And I'm…well, you probably know who I am," I said and flashed my signature smile. Caleb nodded slowly, but my smile didn't seem to work its usual charm. He gestured for me to sit on the chair next to his. *Aaron Remington* the black chair read. I sat down and noticed Caleb had a bunch of writing and highlighting on his script. It looked like he really put a lot of thought into this. I started at my script, which had zero writing besides my name at the top corner in illegible handwriting. Well, I must look fucking professional compared to this go-getter.

"What do you think of the script?" Caleb asked me.

I turned my nose up. "It's okay, for a romance, I guess. Romance isn't usually my thing."

Caleb looked away sharply. "Yeah, I can see that," he muttered.

I narrowed my eyes. *What was that supposed to mean?* I sniffed. "I just meant that, it's not the only thing I can play." Caleb's cheeks flushed at this. I smiled to myself. *Two can play at this game, Caleb Robinson.*

He was about to respond when Melinda shouted, "Alright! We're going to kick filming off with the park scene! Aaron, Caleb, on set please!" My heartbeat quickened. I forgot that films are normally shot out of order. Of course we were starting with the date scene. In that scene, Caleb and I were supposed to be having our first date in the park. I walked up onto the set with my script when Melinda stopped me. "What are you doing with that?" she asked, referring to my script. *Oh. Right.* It was supposed to be memorized. I sighed and tossed the script onto my chair.

Caleb was just staring at me. I glared at him. *What're you looking at?* I thought. I sat on the park bench and Caleb sat next to me. There was fake grass and trees around us, as though we were in an actual park. The film crew were doing last minute activities and touch-ups with makeup when it was finally time to shoot the scene. I took deep breaths. I was in *Moonlight fucking Galaxy.* I could do this.

One of the camera assistants held up the clapperboard and yelled "Scene 32, take one!" Melinda called out "ACTION!" and then the camera was rolling.

Caleb turned to me, his blue eyes glimmering. I was taken aback by the expression on his face. It was the face of someone *in love.* How did he do that so fast? He smiled gently and this did something to me.

"Thank you for taking me here," Caleb said shyly. I blinked in surprise, feeling lightheaded.

"You're...you're welcome?" I said back, not understanding what was happening.

"CUT!" Melinda yelled. "That's not the line! Your line is, 'This is one of my favorite spots to relax!' Not, "You're welcome!"

My face warmed and embarrassment made its way into my body. I was so caught off guard that I fucking forgot what to say. Caleb was looking at me, but I refused to look back at him. I didn't need his sympathy or pity. Melinda yelled for us to try again and said "Action!"

"Thank you for taking me here."

I tried to smile in return, but it came out more like a grimace. "This is one of my favorite spots," I said.

There was a pause and Caleb kept smiling. Did he forget his line too? Maybe we could bask in the embarrassment together.

"TO RELAX!" Melinda shouted at me. "FAVORITE SPOT TO RELAX!"

Oh. I was the one who forgot my fucking line. *Again.* This was gonna be a long day.

"Alright, we're gonna film the breakup scene next!" Melinda shouted.

We were now on a sound stage that was supposed to be my character's home. I sighed, tired, and got into position. I forgot how *grueling* filming can be. Everything moves so fast, and there's little time to ask any questions. Caleb and I sat on the couch that was onstage, and we waited for the call to start.

"Know your lines?" Caleb asked. There was no sarcasm in his voice, but it still irritated me. I looked away.

"Testing me?" I asked. Caleb looked down at his lap. "No. I just figured since the last scene you—"

"Just worry about your own lines," I interrupted.

Caleb went red and clenched his fists. *Good.* Let him be mad. Finally, Melinda was ready to begin, and I saw Caleb take a deep breath and close his eyes.

Melinda yelled "Action!" and the cameras started rolling.

Caleb looked up at me, *tears* in his eyes. What the fuck? *How did he do that so quickly?* I wondered to myself.

"Why are you doing this?" he asked.

I was so surprised I almost forgot my line. *Think, you idiot, think!* "It's too painful to hide our relationship. I need to figure things out. It's not fair to you," I answered.

There. I remembered my lines. Caleb opened his mouth to say his next line, when I heard a loud, "CUT!"

I froze. *What now?* I thought, irritated. Melinda came up to me. "Is there a problem?" I asked. "I recited the correct line," I pointed out.

Melinda sighed and shook her head. "Aaron; It's not enough to recite your line. You have to *mean* it, *feel* it. It's called *acting*. Ever heard of it?" she asked, sarcasm dripping from her tone. I squinted at her. "Let's try again, but this time think about the situation you're in. Let yourself feel how painful this moment is for you. You need to do your acting homework," Melinda said, hands on hips.

I nodded, biting my tongue. *Sure. I'll show you a painful feeling,* I thought bitterly. I could feel Caleb enjoying my lecture and I wanted to hurt him severely. *Little shit,* I thought. I had to admit it, though: the guy is a fantastic actor. I could see why he was Hollywood's current 'it' boy. *And it annoyed the hell out of me.*

CHAPTER 10

Caleb

Filming was going disastrously, to say the least. It was probably the worst start to a shoot I'd ever had in my life. Aaron kept flubbing his lines and he was as stiff as a board. I was trying my best, I really was, but my patience was wearing thin. Not only that, but the asshole started giving me attitude the minute we meet. Now I knew for sure that the rumors about him were true. I could feel Melinda's frustration and I shared it. Aaron was seriously slowing us down. He hadn't had any violent outbursts, but I still hoped he'd be replaced by someone who can actually do his job.

We were on lunch break and I was eating by myself in my trailer. I thought about Remington. He had dark brooding eyes and black hair that was sort of long with sideswept bangs. He had pale skin, as if he were a vampire. He rarely smiled, and in general kept to himself. He was attractive, as much as I hated to admit it. I could see his arm muscles bulging from his T-shirt and I forced myself to stop thinking about that. Aaron Remington was a jerk. Not only that, but he also couldn't even be bothered to properly prepare for this movie. He probably thought of it as a joke. Meanwhile, I'm out here taking this seriously and putting in the effort. It pissed me off thinking about it. I put my lunch away and mustered up the strength to go back to set. I checked the schedule; apparently, we were shooting the dance scene next. I changed into my costume for the scene, a black fitted tuxedo. Of course, Remington was five minutes late from lunch and looked like he got changed in a hurry. Despite this, he still looked dashing in the matching black tuxedo. I shook my head, telling myself to get these thoughts out of my head.

"Okay, everybody! We're gonna try shooting the dance scene now!" Melinda shouted.

I nodded and got into position. Remington seemed a bit lost, so I pointed to the piece of tape where he was supposed to stand. Remington came to stand in front of me.

"I know where to go," he said.

That was a sorry excuse for a thank-you, I thought. Especially when he clearly didn't know what he was doing. In this scene, we were supposed to be at a fancy party. There were a bunch of extras around us, acting as other partygoers. Melinda approached us with another woman I didn't recognize.

"Hi boys, I'm Jo. I'll be your intimacy coach for some scenes in the movie." I nodded; I'd worked with other intimacy coaches before. They basically help with the intimate scenes of films, like sex scenes and whatnot. Which I wasn't looking forward to—at all. I looked at Remington, who looked confused. A little laugh escaped me; of course, he probably didn't know what an intimacy coach even was.

Remington narrowed his eyes. "Something funny?" he asked accusingly. I shook my head, not wanting to start an argument. Jo proceeded to explain her role to us.

"Basically, I'll help choreograph any scenes in the film where there is intimacy, such as close physical contact and scenes of sexual nature." Jo gestured around the set. "For this scene, you two will obviously be dancing and I'll guide you through that. It's nothing complicated, just some basic footwork."

Jo directed me to put my arms around Remington's shoulders, which I did. It wasn't exactly easy since he was significantly taller than I was. Jo told Remington to put his hands on my waist. Remington stiffly nodded and set his hands on me. Then we practiced dancing a bit, just back and forth. Remington seemed to have two left feet, and kept stepping on me. I couldn't tell if he was doing it on purpose or not. Finally, it was time to actually shoot the damn scene. Melinda called action and the scene started.

I looked up at Remington. "May I have this dance?" I asked, holding out my hand.

Remington fumbled his lines again of course, and I couldn't help but feel sorry for him at this point. Eventually, he was able to say his appropriate lines, and we attempted to start dancing.

I guided my arms around Remington's neck, and he put his hands on my waist. We swayed back and forth, and at first it seemed to be actually going alright.

Then Remington stepped on my foot, to which I bit my lip to keep from yelping in pain. He seemed to forget there were extras around us, also dancing, and we accidentally bumped into another couple. This caused them to fall, which created a domino effect. Soon, everyone was falling down. Remington tried to move, but he too stumbled and fell, pulling me with him. You'd think that it couldn't get any worse, but when we fell, we hit the studio lights and they all came crashing down with a big BOOM! The mic also fell down, creating a horrible squealing sound.

And then…Silence.

CHAPTER 11

Aaron

I lay there on the floor of the set with Caleb on top of me. I was at my lowest point, both physically and emotionally.

"Can you please get off me?" I asked. Caleb just glowered at me and slowly got back on his feet. He held out his hand, but I ignored it and got up on my own. I looked around the set; it looked like a hurricane had come through. All the studio lights were toppled on the floor, along with the mic and other set pieces. Luckily, none of the camera equipment seemed to be damaged. At the middle of all of this was Melinda, who was red as a tomato. It would almost be comedic if it weren't for the unfortunate circumstances. I brushed myself off and tried to retain what was left of my dignity. After making sure no one was hurt, Melinda walked over to Caleb and me.

"A word. *In private.*" We trudged behind her and followed her outside. Melinda turned around and crossed her arms.

"This isn't going to work. This has been a *complete* shitshow ever since we started." She looked at me. "You're constantly messing up your lines and are putting in zero effort to have any chemistry. You're stiff as a board and deliver your lines like wood." Caleb was nodding along as she listed my faults. *Little fucker.*

But then, Melinda turned on Caleb. "And *you.*" Caleb's eyes went wide, and he looked shocked. I smiled a little at this, savoring it. "I expected so much more from you after hearing how pleasant you are to work with. How you always give your best performance. I've seen *Bleeding Rose* and I can tell you're not putting in the effort either. I know you can do better."

Caleb looked like he was about to cry. I almost felt bad for him. *Almost.* Melinda shook her head, obviously disappointed in both of us. "I'm gonna need to find replacements for both of you."

Caleb's mouth dropped open and I couldn't blame him. He's obviously never been fired before. I stood there, and...I don't know. A part of me felt like Caleb shouldn't be fired for this. Okay, yeah, I probably should have been fired. But I wanted to salvage the situation, if possible. I did desperately need the money, after all.

"Are you able to give us one more chance?" I asked. Caleb looked at me in shock.

Melinda tilted her head, also surprised. "And why should I? You both have already proven yourselves incompetent."

I nodded in agreement. "I understand that, and you're right. But if we can prove to you that we can put on a good performance, can you give us just one more chance? Please?"

Melinda narrowed her eyes and considered it. She eventually breathed out. "Fine. I'll give you both another chance." Caleb looked completely relieved to hear this. "But," Melinda continued. "You'll have to play by my rules. I want authenticity for this film. And for that to happen, you two *need* to spend some time together. Some *serious* quality time *bonding*. Otherwise, this movie won't survive."

I gaped. Was Melinda serious? I had to hang out and *bond* with this guy who clearly hates me? Melinda raised an eyebrow. "Is that a problem?" she asked.

I shook my head, not wanting to make her angry again.

Melinda squinted. "That's what I thought. So, here's what's gonna happen. I'm gonna compile a list of activities for you guys to do together. You both need to figure your shit out and develop your relationships. And once we resume filming, I better see a huge difference. Otherwise, you're both fired. Is that clear?"

Melinda waited for our answers. Caleb spoke up first. "I understand. Thank you so much for giving me-*us*-another chance. We won't let you down."

Melinda nodded in response and then told us to scram. I guess that meant we had the rest of the day off. I turned to head back to the parking lot, when I heard Caleb say, "Aaron, wait." I stopped in my tracks but didn't turn around. "Um...I just wanted to say thanks. For convincing Melinda to not fire us." I didn't know how to respond. Why the fuck was this guy *thanking* me? He should be pissed at me for almost getting him fired in the first place.

"I was doing it for me, not you," I finally said. "I need to do this movie for private reasons." Then I walked away, without waiting to hear his response.

"You. Fucking. *Bitch*," I yelled over the phone.

"Um...hello to you too?" Tracy said on the other end.

"This is all your fault! I should have *known* you were behind this!"

I could hear Tracy laughing. "Uh, oh. So the cat's out of the bag, huh?"

I shook my head even though I knew she couldn't see me. "Because of your meddling, I'm now stuck doing a gay romance film with Caleb Robinson *and* I fucked things up like I always do!"

Tracy sighed. "I was doing this to *help* you."

"How is *embarrassing* me helping me?!" I shouted.

Tracy clicked her tongue. "I got you the part because I know you really needed the money. And I thought it could help mend your reputation and relaunch your acting career. I was *trying* to be a good friend."

I was silent for a moment. When she put it that way, it really did sound like Tracy cared about my well-being. "Oh. Well...thanks, I guess. But I completely made a fool of myself on set! And now I'm forced to spend a week with Caleb Robinson!" I groaned.

"Oh, get over it. Be grateful you didn't get fired and just put up with it. I'm sure it won't be as bad as you're making it out to be."

"If things don't work out, I'm blaming you, Tracy!" I exclaimed.

All I could hear was Tracy laughing wildly as she said goodbye and hung up. I stared at the phone in amazement. Tracy really was something else. Then I felt a buzz on my phone. An email from...Melinda. *Oh no.* I tapped the email:

Hello, boys. Here is the list of activities you'll be doing together to strengthen your relationship. I'll send you

*another email once we resume filming. Remember if
you don't improve, you're both fired!*

Have fun!

Melinda

There was a schedule attached. I tapped on it which
led me to this:

WHO?	WHAT?	WHERE?	WHEN?
Aaron & Caleb	Bowling	Lucky Strike LA	Monday
Aaron & Caleb	Aquarium	Aquarium of the Pacific, Long Beach	Tuesday
Aaron & Caleb	Arcade	EightyTwo, LA	Wednesday
Aaron & Caleb	Karaoke	Shrine Room, LA	Thursday
Aaron & Caleb	Picnic	Your choice	Friday

Fuck. I was *not* looking forward to this week.

CHAPTER 12

Caleb

Monday

I stared at the time on my phone. It was 12:15 p.m. Remington was fifteen minutes late for our first activity. I should have figured. I sighed to myself and looked around the bowling alley, Lucky Strike. There were neon lights flashing everywhere, and it was *loud*. A lot of people like bowling, it turns out. I was about to give up and head home, when lo and behold, Remington walked up. He was wearing a black trench coat with black jeans and combat boots. His black hair is covered in a gray beanie, and he wore dark sunglasses. He looked like a model. He just nodded at me, and we both just sort of stood there awkwardly.

"Well," Aaron finally said. "Let's just get this over with, shall we?" He walked over to reserve a lane. I followed him and we picked out a lane that was away from the other groups. I entered our names and turned to Aaron who was walking away.

"Just going to get a drink," he said. I shook my head and sat down. This was not how I wanted to spend my day. Eventually, Aaron came back holding two drinks. He just jutted his arm out at me, holding the drink. I cautiously took it.

"Thanks," I said. I took a sip and wow, it was *strong*, whatever it was. I couldn't help but cough and Aaron, for the first time, smiled. It was a dashing smile.

"Too strong?" He asked.

I collected myself. "A little," I replied, setting the drink down. "Shall we start?" I asked.

Aaron raised his glass. "After you, my good man." I grabbed a bowling ball and tried to focus. I can't even remember the last time I went bowling. I swung my arm back and forth before releasing the ball. I watched as it slowly rolled…into the gutter, knocking zero pins over. I could hear Remington slowly clapping.

"Wow. That was great." I turned around, wanting to throw a bowling ball at him.

"Alright then, let's see how *you* do."

Aaron smirked and set his glass down. "Watch how a pro does it," he said as he grabbed a bowling ball and threw it down. It rolled swiftly across the lane before knocking all ten pins down. I gaped; *was this guy for real?* Aaron turned around, obviously pleased with himself.

"That was just beginner's luck," I sputtered.

Aaron sat back down. "Keep telling yourself that, buddy."

I stood up, wanting to prove myself. I grabbed a ball, and I focused as hard as I could. I threw the bowling ball, but this time it bounced up and down before once again going off the track. *Are you fucking kidding me?* I went to sit down, when Remington stood up and walked over to me with a bowling ball. He handed me the ball and looked at me.

"Now, pretend like you're gonna throw it," he said. I eyed him suspiciously but did as I was told. Remington stopped me. "First, you need to straighten your wrist. Then, you need to hold the ball close to your ankles." He put his hand on my shoulder and guided me as I threw the ball. This time, the ball rolled down a straight line and knocked most of the pins over. Aaron grinned, and it wasn't his usual sarcastic grin. This was a genuine grin, all his white teeth showing. Something in me made my heart skip a beat.

"See? I knew you could do it!" Remington said.

I blushed and looked down. "T-thanks," I muttered.

He stared at me. "No problem."

We both sat back down, sipping our drinks. "If you want, I can help you with your lines," I told Aaron.

He narrowed his eyes. "Why? Because I keep fucking them up?" he asked.

My eyes widened. "N-no, I just thought it might help—"

Aaron cut me off. "Look. I don't need your help. I've been in the business since I was a child. Yeah, my gears need some oiling, but I'm not a novice," he said sharply.

I looked down at my drink, shaking. I was beginning to think Remington had more layers, but obviously he was just a self-entitled prick like I thought. I nodded towards the lane.

"You're up." Remington sighed and rolled the ball, knocking all the pins down once again. In the end, Remington won of course. We both walked towards the exit, and I turned to Remington.

"Well. I guess I'll see you tomorrow for the aquarium?" He nodded, and we went our separate ways. As I walked away I turned to have one last look at Remington. *What a strange guy.*

"So how did the bowling date go?" Lucy asked. It was later that day, and we were watching some Matt Damon action movie at my apartment. I shrugged, eating popcorn.

"It was alright. Turns out, I suck at bowling."

Lucy laughed. "But how was Aaron?"

I thought for a minute. "Aaron…is a strange one. It's almost like he lacks social skills or something."

Lucy tilted her head. "In what way?" she asked.

I stared at the screen. "Like, one minute he's trying to help me bowl but then he acts like an ass again the next minute."

Lucy nodded. "Maybe he's just insecure?"

I barked out a laugh. "Uh, more like the opposite. The guy is full of himself!"

Lucy shrugged. "Sometimes people act like they're confident when they're just insecure about themselves."

She did have a point. Could that be the case for Remington? I wasn't sure. "We're supposed to go to the aquarium tomorrow. I'm just worried that we still won't be able to give good performances when we resume filming."

Lucy took some popcorn from the bowl. "Just see how it plays out until Friday. You never know; he could end up being a good friend or something."

I had to laugh at this. Remington and me? *Good friends*?

Yeah, right.

CHAPTER 13

Aaron

Tuesday

When I pulled up to the parking lot, I spotted Caleb waiting by the entrance. I pulled my beanie down over my head and made sure I had my dark sunglasses so no one would recognize me. Caleb must have been thinking the same thing. He was wearing an Angels baseball cap and dark shades as well. I walked over and nodded at him. We went to buy our tickets and I handed some money to the cashier.

"Two tickets, please," I said. Caleb tugged on my sleeve.

"You don't have to—" I waved my hand.

"It's fine, really."

Caleb nodded his thanks. We walked into the aquarium together and...wow. There were shades of blue everywhere; glass tanks lined the walls with clear water, and various sea creatures swam around. There were colorful fishes, lobters, eels, and even some seahorses.

"What do you want to do?" Caleb asked.

I shrugged. "You pick."

Caleb looked at the directory. "Hmm…how do you feel about the shark lagoon?" he asked. I froze. The truth was, I hated sharks. They made me feel uneasy. I couldn't let Caleb know this, so I nodded. We made our way into the shark exhibit, where we were surrounded by glass walls, behind which there were several types of sharks swimming around. I could see hammerhead sharks and tiger sharks among others. I stiffened and tried to stare straight ahead. *How was this legal?* I thought.

"You alright?" Caleb asked. I gave him the side-eye.

"Why?"

Caleb shrugged. "You just seem…tense." I was silent, and then understanding seemed to wash over him.

"Oh…are you…*scared* of sharks?" he asked in amazement.

I sharply turned away. "I'm not *scared*…they just make me uncomfortable." Then the bastard started laughing. "It's not funny," I narrowed my eyes.

"Sorry," Caleb said, stopping his laughter. "I wasn't laughing at you, I promise. I just thought…" he stopped.

"Thought what?"

"I just thought that the great Aaron Remington wasn't afraid of, well, *anything*." I smiled a little to myself.

"For the most part, I'm not. I guess everyone has at least one thing they're afraid of, though," I said. Caleb nodded and started to walk away.

"Let's go to the coral reefs. There's some neat animals there!" I followed him, grateful to be away from the sharks. We went to the coral reefs where there were different animals. There were more colorful fish swimming around and even some sea turtles.

"Look, there's Nemo!" Caleb pointed excitedly at a clownfish. I smirked; it was kind of cute the way he got all excited, like a little kid. I stared at the fishes; I had to admit, it had a calming effect on me.

"You know, I've never been to an aquarium," I said.

Caleb gaped at me. "What? You've never been? Not even with family?" I shook my head. Caleb looked at the glass. "I used to go to the aquarium with my family a lot when I was younger." He looked wistful.

I shoved my hands in my pockets. "My parents never really took my sister and I on outings like this…they were always busy with work. Never really had time for either of us," I said. I frowned. Why was I telling him all this? Caleb looked at me with sympathy, but I turned away.

"Have you always wanted to be an actor?" he asked suddenly. *Had* I? I wasn't sure. Really, my parents just started submitting me for roles, and I just went with it because it made them happy. I knew they wanted to have a *star* for a son.

"No," I finally said. "I didn't ever want to be one. I just sort of did it because...my parents expected me to do it."

Caleb nodded slowly. "Do you enjoy it?" he asked.

I shrugged. "I mean, I don't *hate* it...but it probably wouldn't have been what I would have chosen."

Caleb softly tapped the glass. "What would you choose, if you could be anything you wanted?"

I thought for a moment. "I think I would have liked teaching. Maybe English or something. I always enjoyed books and reading."

There was some silence. I looked at Caleb. "What about you?" I pressed. "Did you always want to act?"

Caleb nodded. "It's been my dream since I was a kid. I always loved performing. I was in the school plays and all that." I stared at Caleb's side profile; the way the blue water reflected cast a magical glow on him, and something about it was hauntingly beautiful—like he was in a painting.

"Your dreams came true," I observed. Caleb blushed and shrugged modestly. "Was it everything you thought it would be?" I asked.

Caleb paused. "I think so..." Caleb started and then stopped. He frowned a little.

"There's a but, isn't there?" I said knowingly.

Caleb breathed out shakily and looked at the floor. "Do you…ever feel like your whole life is a performance? Like, you're acting all the time and always putting on a show for everyone, hiding things about yourself?" he asked hesitantly.

I snorted. "That's show business for you." I looked at Caleb; I wished he wasn't wearing sunglasses so I could see his blue eyes. "Everyone hides something. No one really knows who we are, not really. We're acting all the time, being a different character with different people. That's life," I finished.

Caleb looked up at me. "Yeah," he said. "You're right."

I swallowed; I felt a magnetic pull between us as the water casted shadows all around us.

"I'm…" Caleb started. I waited for him to continue but he looked away. "Do you want to visit the gift shop?" he asked finally. I had a feeling he wanted to say something else, but I didn't press him on it. I just nodded and we made our way to the shop. It was filled with sea-themed merchandise; key chains, shirts, jewelry, stuffed animals. Caleb hurried to the stuffed animals and picked up a sea turtle.

"Oh, how cute!" he exclaimed. I smiled; he really was like a little kid. Caleb set the turtle down and excused himself to the restroom. I picked up the sea turtle. I don't know what possessed me to do this, but I bought it while he was gone. *What the fuck was I doing?* It's not like we were friends, but a part of me wanted to see that smile again. There was something wrong with me, truly. I stood in a corner, until Caleb eventually returned. He crinkled his brow.

"What's that?" he asked, looking at the giftbag. I didn't know what to say, so I just held it out to him. He tentatively took the bag and peered inside. He laughed as he pulled the turtle out.

"You didn't have to get me this!" Caleb said. I shrugged and Caleb reached for his wallet.

"At least let me pay you back!"

I shook my head. "Consider it a thank you."

Caleb cocked his head. "For what?"

"I don't know. For not making fun of me for being afraid of sharks."

Caleb laughed again. "Alright, I'll accept it. Thank you." He looked up at me and smiled, and it did something to me. Was it worth it? Maybe just a little.

CHAPTER 14

Caleb

When I got back to my apartment, I collapsed on the couch. I was tired and was glad to be home. I thought about the aquarium and Remington. It was an interesting day to say the least. Remington seemed to open up a little and was surprisingly…insightful? I picked up the giftbag and took the turtle out, staring at it. I was unsure what the meaning behind this gift was, but it was thoughtful of Aaron. I decided I would name it Remy, after Remington. I laughed to myself and put the turtle on my shelf. Maybe Lucy was right. Maybe we *could* be friends. I frowned. No, he was only hanging out with me because he had to. Not because he *wanted* to, I reminded myself. I was about to turn on the TV when my phone buzzed. It was a text from Brent. My insides flipped. I had almost forgotten about him. It read:

Hey. Wanna come over?

I hesitated. It was probably a bad idea. I started to type that I couldn't when another text came in.

I promise I'll make it worth ur while

Maybe I could spare an hour or two.

We fell back onto the bed, both panting. We were covered in sweat and cum, both in a post-orgasm haze. After a minute, Brent was looking at me, as if waiting for something. *Oh, right.* It was time to sneak out the back. I cleaned myself up and was about to head out when something stopped me in my tracks. I turned to Brent, who was still lying naked on the bed.

"Brent," I started. He nodded, waiting for me to go on. "Don't you…ever get tired? Of hiding?"

Brent shrugged, like it wasn't a big deal. "Where's this coming from?" he asked.

I looked at the floor. "It's just…don't you want to have something *real*? Something you don't hide, something with *substance*?"

Brent just stared at me. "I'm happy with the way things are. I'm not looking to get married or shit like that, if that's what you mean. I mean…you didn't really expect us to become boyfriends and ride off into the sunset, did you?"

Although Brent laughed as he said this, it still felt like a punch in the gut. Anger and sadness welled up inside me. I laughed it off and nodded.

"Of course not. I'll see you around, Brent," I said and walked away. I was a fucking fool.

Wednesday

Eventually, tomorrow came around and it was time for the arcade. After the whole thing with Brent, I just wanted to stay home and sulk. But I knew I didn't have a choice. I put on my baseball cap, sunglasses, and headed out. It was sunny outside and as I pulled up to the arcade, I could see the lot was almost empty. Which made sense, I guess. It was the middle of the week, after all. I waited near the entrance and eventually I saw Remington's familiar tall frame walk up. We walked in and there was…no one there, besides a bartender and a bored-looking girl attending the prize area. We bought some coins and decided to play a racing game. Of course, Remington beat me with little effort. I shook my head in amazement.

"How do you do that?" I asked him.

"Do what?"

"Be good at *everything!*" I exclaimed.

Aaron snickered. "Trust me, I'm not. I tend to fuck up everything." I wondered what he meant by this, but I didn't ask. We just sat there in the racing chairs, the game music covering up the silence. Something's been nagging at me and so I decided to just ask.

"Hey...why did you agree to do this movie in the first place?" I asked. Aaron didn't say anything for a moment. I looked at him, and wondered if I asked the wrong question. "I just mean...you don't seem very fond of romance movies. It doesn't seem like your style." He sighed and leaned back in the arcade chair.

"You've...probably heard things about me, I'm assuming. Not so great things. You also probably have heard about Aaron Remington's famous public meltdown." I looked away. I had seen the video, and it was...something. Watching him scream and yell at the restaurant staff and then the paparazzi, telling them to fuck off. Throwing food at them.

"What...happened? If you don't mind me asking," I quietly asked.

Aaron was quiet and looked away. "I thought I was invincible. Like I was Superman. I thought no one could touch me, and that I was above everybody else." He rubbed his face with his hands. "I became addicted to the celebrity life. Alcohol, drugs, sex. You name it. That day, I had gotten into some stupid argument with my sister. She hates me, but that's beside the point. I had gotten drunk at the restaurant; the waiter got my order wrong…" Remington shook his head. "The paparazzi came, which just added fuel to the fire. It's all so pathetic." I was quiet, not knowing what to say. Aaron looked lost in thought. "Maybe they were right," he said, more to himself than to me. "Maybe it really *is* the end for me." I breathed out and stared hard at Aaron.

"Aaron, look. I know I don't know you very well…and I'll admit, before we met, I had a lot of…predispositions about you." I shifted in my seat. "We all make mistakes. We all do bad things. It doesn't mean we're bad *people*. And, looking at you today…I can tell you're not a bad person." I held my breath, waiting for Remington's response. He just looked at me, his face unreadable.

"How can you be so sure?"

"Because…bad people don't help other people bowl. And they *definitely* don't buy stuffed animals for other people, either." Remington smiled a little, which made me happy. He nodded gently.

"Well…I'm still not sure I believe you. But I'll take that into consideration," he said. A little bit of silence passed before Remington spoke up. "I went on a tangent there. I never answered your question. I'm doing this movie in hopes it will somewhat mend my career and reputation. I need the money, too."

I nodded in response. "Oh…well, I hope it works out for you."

"What about you? Why did you decided to do this gay romance movie?" My heartbeat quickened and my palms got clammy. I had to tread carefully.

"My agent thought it would be a good idea," I said. Which wasn't a lie. "Apparently, some people believe my movies are getting stale and this would be a way to mix things up."

"I see. And is that it?" he asked.

I froze. "Yeah. Yeah, that's it," I finally said. We got up from our seats and tried playing a game where you have to shoot zombies. I couldn't shoot well, so Remington killed most of them for me. We decided to end it there and head for the parking lot. It had turned dark already to my surprise. I turned to say goodbye to Remington, not realizing he was right behind me, and I bumped into his chest.

"Sorry," I said and tried to pull away, but Remington held onto my arms. I looked up in confusion and Remington stared down at me. My heartbeat quickened and he took my sunglasses off. He stared into my eyes hungrily.

Then he kissed me.

CHAPTER 15

Aaron

I don't know why I did it. I don't know what came over me. When Caleb bumped into me, and I caught him…I could see his cheeks were red from the cold. I could count all the moles on his face. I wanted to desperately see those clear blue eyes again. It was like I wasn't in control of my body. Before I knew it, I was staring into those ocean eyes. I leaned down, and I pressed my lips to his. I closed my eyes and basked in the moment, savoring it. Then Caleb pulled back and stared at me, all wide-eyed and in complete shock. Reality came crashing back. *Oh shit. What have I done?* I took a step backwards.

"I-I'm sorry," I stuttered. "I… shouldn't have done that." Caleb opened his mouth, but I was already running back to my car and then I drove off, leaving him standing there. *What the fuck is wrong with me?*

I drove as fast as I could back home, jammed the key in the door, and slammed it shut. I went into my room, closed the door, and flopped face down on the bed.

"Fucking stupid," I shouted into my pillow. *How did I manage to fuck up everything in my life? How was it possible?* Before I knew it, I was crying. It was time for a drink. I went into the kitchen and cracked open a can of Mike's Hard Lemonade. I took a long swig and then I felt a little better. I wiped my tears with my hand and washed my face. I looked at my phone to see if there were any messages from Caleb, but there were none. Of course there weren't. Why would he message me after I kissed him out of nowhere? The dude is probably straight and now thinks I'm some perverted weirdo who got the wrong idea. He probably would want to film the movie with someone else, not that I blame him. I lit a cigarette and took a sharp drag. I blew the smoke out, and realized my family was right. I really was a fuck-up.

Thursday

"You did what?!" Tracy screamed into the phone. I winced and pulled the phone away from my ear.

"Why in the world would you kiss him?! I thought you hated him!" she continued.

I sighed. "I do. I mean…I think I do. I don't know. I'm confused," I admitted.

Tracy scoffed. "Clearly. So, what did Caleb say after you fucking kissed him?"

I was silent for a moment. I sniffed and then said, "I sort of…drove away before he could say anything."

Silence. "What the fuck is wrong with you?!" Tracy finally yelled into the phone. I winced again.

"Can you please stop bursting my eardrum?" I asked her.

"I'll stop when you stop making dumbass decisions!" Tracy exclaimed.

I paced the hallway. "I don't know. I wasn't thinking. It was like I was possessed. I couldn't think straight, and then I just ran away. Like I usually do when I fuck up."

Tracy sighed. "So, what are you gonna do now?"

I thought for a moment. "I should probably apologize. He hasn't texted me at all, and I doubt he's gonna go to our karaoke outing today after this."

"You can't just leave things like this. It's not fair to you or him. You need to talk to him again, whether it's on the phone or in person."

I knew Tracy was right. I had to fix things. I looked at my phone. It was one o'clock. We were supposed to meet at 12:30. He probably didn't show up at all, and if he did, he's probably left by now. Only one way to find out.

I drove as fast as I could towards The Shrine Room, an Egyptian themed karaoke bar. I jumped out of the car and ran into the place. I looked around; it was dimly lit and there were statues of mummies and sarcophagi everywhere. I ran to the woman at the front podium.

"Has a guy come here today? On the shorter side, probably wearing a baseball cap and dark sunglasses?"

The woman looked taken aback. "Yes, I think he's in one of our karaoke rooms."

"Which room?" I pressed.

She looked at her tablet. "Um…I think he's in our Mummy Hall, which is located upstairs—" I didn't wait for her to finish. I ran upstairs and looked around before seeing a room with a mummy carved onto the door. I barged in and… there he was. Caleb. Sitting on one of the couches, staring at the karaoke screen. Caleb jumped in fright and looked at me in surprise.

"You're still here," I said breathlessly.

Caleb nodded slowly. "Yeah. I didn't think you were gonna show up."

I put my hands on my hips, panting. "I… wanted to apologize." Caleb was silent, waiting for me to go on. "I shouldn't have kissed you like that. And I definitely shouldn't have run away after kissing you. I'm…sorry."

Caleb sighed and looked down. "I… don't know what to say."

I nodded. "That's alright. You don't have to say anything. I understand if you don't want to do the movie anymore. Or if you want me recast. After all, I overstepped our boundaries."

Caleb stayed silent. "I didn't know you were gay," he finally said.

I stared at him, confused. *That's* what he cared about? "I'm bi, actually," I clarified.

Caleb nodded. "I guess there's no harm in telling you, then. I'm gay. I just keep it a secret from everyone because I'm afraid it will ruin my career."

I blinked in surprise. *Oh.* "I won't tell anyone," I reassured him. Caleb smiled sweetly in response. I looked around the room. "Well, we're already here. Might as well make the most of it, right?"

CHAPTER 16

Caleb

So Aaron and I decided to stay and sing some karaoke since the room was already booked. I sang *Landslide* by Fleetwood Mac, and Aaron did a pretty good Elvis imitation and sang *Can't Help Falling in Love.* I had to admit, it might have made me swoon a little. I laughed at his Elvis impression, and we sang some more songs. As we wrapped things up, Aaron looked at me.

"Would you want to come over? I figured maybe we could practice our lines or something."

I nodded. "Yeah, that sounds good."

Aaron nodded back to me. "Cool. You can follow me there," he said. We went into the parking lot and I followed Aaron to his house. As we got there, I had the same feeling I had when visiting Alison's house. Amazement. His house was like a mansion, painted white with an open balcony and red-tiled roof. Aaron led me inside, and I looked around.

"So this is where the famous Aaron Remington lives," I observed. Aaron shrugged, as if it were no big deal. We sat down at his kitchen table after Aaron poured us some drinks.

"You said you came to the aquarium a lot with your family. Are you guys close?" Aaron asked.

I nodded. "Yeah, I sort of come from a big family. They were always supportive of me wanting to become an actor. We're all pretty tight. There's never a dull moment when we're all together."

Aaron slowly nodded. "That must be nice. I'm more used to just being in this big empty house all the time," he admitted. I felt bad for Aaron; he had mentioned before how he was never close with his own family. Aaron shook his head. "Sorry, I wasn't trying to dampen the mood."

I took a sip from my drink. "It's fine. Don't worry about it," I said. "Does...does your family know about you being gay?" Aaron asked hesitantly.

"Yeah, they do. And they're all supportive about it. They know I don't want anyone else knowing so they keep my secret for me."

Aaron sipped from his glass. "Well, that's good you have your family's support," he said. I tapped the edge of the table, wanting to know more about Aaron.

"Does your family know about you?" I asked.

He scoffed and shook his head. "If anything, it would probably just be an imperfection to them," he said.

I frowned, anger welling in me. "That's not an imperfection. It isn't even something you control!" I yelled without meaning to.

Aaron shrugged. "Try telling that to my parents," he said. Some silence passed before Aaron spoke up. "Is it alright if I show you something?" he asked. I nodded and he stood up and started walking. I followed him down the hall to a room in the back of the house. Aaron took out a key and opened the door. We went inside and the lights flickered on. It seemed to be some sort of...storage room. With memorabilia of *Moonlight Galaxy* everywhere. Posters, toys, shirts, various other merchandise. The room was huge, every wall covered with a framed poster from the various movies.

"Wow," I said. Aaron nodded, looking around as well. I walked over and picked up a gold trophy. *Best Child Actor in a Science-Fiction Film*. There were other awards, like Golden Globes and Emmy's.

"I call this my trophy room," Aaron explained. "Now, I'm considering changing the name to my shame room," he continued. I set the trophy down and looked at him in confusion.

"*Shame*? But...this room shows nothing but success!" I exclaimed.

Aaron shook his head. "My success from the *past*. Now, I'm just a washed-up celebrity whose known for flipping out on waiters." He took off a framed poster and opened a little compartment. He pulled out a piece of crumpled paper and handed it to me. I unfolded it. It was an old tabloid article detailing Aaron's public meltdown. I handed the article back to Aaron and looked at him in his dark eyes.

"You can't keep living in the past, Aaron. Your past doesn't define you. You get to decide that." Aaron was silent as he put the article back into the compartment.

"It's easier said than done," he replied. He was silent for a moment. "I've never let anyone into this room before," he admitted. I looked around, feeling special that Aaron brought me here.

"Thank you," I said. "For trusting me." Aaron stood in front of me, and I looked up at him.

"You're welcome," he whispered. I stood up on my toes, and I kissed him. I could feel the scruff of his facial hair and smell the scent of his aftershave. He kissed me back and wrapped his arms around my waist. I put my hands on his face and kissed him harder. We went on like this, before we pulled back, both of us panting.

"Wanna go to my room?" Aaron asked. I knew what this meant, and I didn't hesitate to say yes. He took my hand and led me to his room. I turned to look at him and he looked down at me, with yearning in his eyes. I could see the faint freckles on his pale skin, and his dark stubble carved down his defined cheekbones. He touched my face with his hand, and slowly leaned in to kiss me. I closed my eyes, and I felt his tongue tentatively enter my mouth. I opened wider, inviting him in. I explored his mouth with my tongue and ran my hands down his dark curls. He put his hands under my shirt and caressed my back, pulling me in closer. I lifted my arms and he pulled off my shirt. He ran his hands up and down my chest and abs, and I shivered at the touch.

I wanted to see him shirtless, too. I tugged at his shirt and he took it off. *Wow.* If I wasn't hard already, I definitely was now. I'd expected him to be muscular from his tight shirts, but this was something else. He had a defined, round chest with hair covering his dark nipples. He had a dark happy trail leading from his rock-hard abs, then disappearing underneath his pants. When I looked closer, I was shocked to see that his nipples were pierced. *Holy shit.* He saw me gaping and grinned. He led me to his bed and pulled me on top of him. We resumed kissing, both shirtless, and I rubbed his chest, feeling the metal piercings on my skin. I could feel his erection press against me, and it turned me the fuck on. I palmed his erection through his pants and he groaned in response. I wanted his dick and I wanted it *now.*

I undid his belt buckle as I kissed him and then started pressing kisses to his chest. I licked and sucked on his nipples, playing with the barbell piercings which Aaron seemed to really enjoy. I then lowered myself level with his crotch. I unzipped his pants and pulled them down, revealing his black boxer briefs. There was a huge tent in his boxers, with a wet spot at the tip. He was already leaking pre-cum, which excited me. I pulled his underwear down, and his cock sprung out, almost hitting me in the face. I licked my lips in anticipation. Aaron was *hung*, which didn't surprise me. His cock was pale, like the color of his skin, with a light pink mushroom head. His pubes were black and wild, and it was so *masculine*.

I grasped his cock with my hand and rubbed my thumb over the head, swiping over the precum. I could hear Aaron breathing heavily, trying to control himself. I licked my thumb and lowered my mouth onto his cock, focusing on the head. I dug my tongue into the slit and then wrapped my lips around his cock, bobbing my head up and down slowly. Aarons hips buckled in response.

"*Fuck*," he groaned. I moved my head up and down on his dick, trying to take in his full length. I played with his large balls with my hand as I did this, and then pressed my face to his pubes. I pulled off and began sucking him faster. I could feel Aaron put his hand on the back of my head, encouraging me to keep going. We went on like this, and I inhaled his masculine musk, intoxicating my senses. After a moment, he told me to stop. I pulled off with a pop, and looked up at him, my lips red and swollen. He looked at me hungrily, as though I was the prey and he was a predator. It was like he was becoming a different person, another beast entirely.

"I wanna fuck you silly," he said.

I nodded in response. Yes. *Yes,* I wanted that too.

"Strip," Aaron ordered. I nodded and took off my pants and underwear, my own hard cock popping out. "Lay face down on the bed," Aaron said. I quickly did as I was told. Aaron stood up, and inspected me, running his hand down my back to my ass. "Fuck, your ass is beautiful," he said, giving it a playful slap. He got on the bed and lowered his face to my ass, pressing soft kisses to my cheeks. And then, he spread my ass, and I could feel his tongue lapping at my hole. *Oh fuck.* He sucked and licked at my pink hole, as if he were starving and it was his last meal on earth. It felt fucking *amazing.* He pressed a couple of more kisses to my ass before stopping. I could hear him take off his pants completely and my heart drummed in excitement. I heard other things like a bottle uncapping and a condom unwrapping. He got on the bed with his knees and told me to turn around and lay on my back. I did, and I could see Aaron towering over me with his huge cock covered in a condom. He grabbed the undersides of my thighs and pulled me down, spreading my legs and putting my feet over his shoulders. I breathed heavily, not feeling real. I could feel the blunt tip of his cock begin to enter me, splitting my sides apart. I groaned, reveling in the pain and pleasure. He pushed in further, until his full length was inside me. There was complete stillness for a moment.

Then Aaron pulled halfway out and slammed back into me, thrusting in and out. I cried out and he pounded into me relentlessly, holding onto my ankles. He began kissing and sucking on my toes as he drilled me, and *god* I felt like I was in another universe. How was this man even real? This was nothing like being with Brent. This was…something else entirely. He leaned in and kissed me hard on the mouth as he fucked me. Our tongues smashed into each other, and Aaron kept crashing into me, pounding into my prostate. Then, as we kissed, he slowly pulled out.

"Get on your hands and knees," he told me. I quickly obeyed, and Aaron wasted no time shoving his cock back into me. He put his hand on my shoulders and pulled on my hair as he thrusted into me.

"Fuck!" I shouted. He spanked my ass a couple times as he fucked me, and I felt so high.

"You fucking like that?" he growled as he pounded me.

"I fucking love it," I cried out. Aaron's thrusts were getting faster, more urgent. I knew he was close.

"Fuck, I'm gonna come deep in your ass!" he yelled. I could feel his cock begin to make contractions and he groaned, coming inside me. Aaron collapsed onto me and breathed heavily. We both just lay there, panting together. Eventually, Aaron pulled out, removing the condom, and pressed soft kisses on my back.

"Are you alright?" he asked with concern.

I nodded and flipped over onto my back. "That was...fucking incredible," I admitted.

Aaron grinned and I laughed. "Too rough?" he asked.

I shook my head. "No... you were perfect," I said. Aaron lay back on the bed, next to me.

"I haven't had sex like that in... I don't even remember," he said.

"Me either," I said.

Then Aaron noticed my cock, still half hard. "I gotta take care of that," he said lowering himself onto my crotch. I shook my head in protest.

"You don't have to. I just wanted to make you feel good," I said.

Aaron smiled. "Just let me do my thing," he said.

He wrapped his lips around my shaft and fondled my balls, and *fuck* it felt good. He bobbed his head up and down, deepthroating my entire length in one swoop. My feet twitched in response, and it was not long before I came, spilling my cum into Aaron's mouth. He swallowed every last drop, of course. Aaron kissed the head of my cock before lying next to me again. I breathed out.

"You seriously are good at everything," I said. Aaron laughed out loud and then we were both laughing. I could feel myself getting sleepy and the post-orgasm haze wasn't helping. I tried to get up to leave, when Aaron pulled on my arm.

"Stay the night?" he asked, his dark eyes pleading. *How could I say no to that?*

CHAPTER 17

Aaron

Friday

A bit of sunlight peeked through the curtains as I softly opened my eyes. I looked around, unsure of where I was for a moment. I felt a bit delirious. Then I noticed that someone had their arms wrapped around my waist and I looked next to me. Lying there, still asleep, was Caleb Robinson. Then, memories slowly started coming back to me. *We had sex.* Oh fuck.

I looked at Caleb; he was breathing softly, and his blond hair was tousled. It was an adorable look on him—so innocent and tranquil. I smiled to myself. If only I could wake up to this sight *every morning*. That would be something. Caleb shifted and then woke up, and I could see speckles of gray in his blue eyes. He smiled shyly at me.

"Hi," he said.

"Hi," I replied.

"What time is it?" Caleb asked.

I looked at my phone. "It's gonna be nine," I said.

Caleb nodded and lay on his back. I stared at the ceiling, unsure of how I ended up in this situation. I looked at Caleb and grinned.

"Wanna have a picnic?"

We decided to go to Griffith Park and packed lunch together. It was a beautiful day in Los Angeles, all bright and sunny. We found a nice shady spot, and there weren't a lot of people which was nice. Caleb spread a blanket over the grass, and we sat down, unpacking the lunch. We brought sandwiches, soda, deviled eggs, watermelon, and some cookies. Caleb took a bite of his sandwich.

"It's so nice out," he said in between bites. I nodded in agreement and started eating my sandwich.

"You know, I watched one of your movies."

Caleb looked at me in shock. "You did? I thought you hated romance though!"

I shrugged. "I do. But I was curious. And I admit, I was becoming enthralled. I think it had to do with your acting skills, though."

Caleb blushed and looked down, which was the cutest thing ever. "I'm not *that* good," he said modestly.

I put down my sandwich. "Are you kidding? You have this weird superpower where you can act like you're in love automatically. It's freaky," I admitted.

Caleb laughed and shook his head. "I'll admit something. I haven't seen a single *Moonlight Galaxy* movie."

Now it was my turn to gape. "What?! That's like a classic piece of cinema!"

Caleb shrugged. "I was never really into science fiction," he said.

I shook my head in amazement. "Those movies are classic. You're missing out." I paused. "Although, according to my sister, they're shitty." Caleb took a sip of soda and looked at me.

"You said before that you and your sister didn't get along. How come?" he asked.

I sighed and looked at the sky. "I don't know. I guess I got a big head and she didn't like that. She didn't like the person I was becoming. I don't blame her," I said.

Caleb stared at me, the wind gently rustling his hair. "I like the person you are."

My heart skipped a beat. How can he say stuff like that so casually? I took a piece of watermelon and bit into it. Some silence went by as we ate.

Caleb reached for some cookies when he asked, "Aaron…you stayed in rehab, didn't you?" I looked up, surprised by this sudden question.

"I was there for a bit, yeah," I admitted. Caleb looked down.

"What was…it like?" he asked imploringly.

I sighed and thought about it. "It… helped, in some ways. Not so much, in other ways. It was very isolating and gave me a lot of time to think." I took a swig from my drink. "It didn't help much with…my drinking. I still drink a lot," I confessed. "But that's because I didn't really take it seriously." I breathed out. "It did give me time to reflect on myself and my actions. So that was good, I guess."

Caleb nodded and looked around. "I think that…it was brave for you to go," he said.

I laughed sarcastically. "I didn't have much of a choice. My family and my agent threatened to drop me if I didn't."

Caleb shrugged. "I think it's still brave." I stared at him. *What an interesting character*, I thought. No one has ever said things like that to me before.

"You know," Caleb said. "I just realized. You don't have to hang out with me again after this." I looked at him, confused. He took a bite of his cookie. "Today's our last mandatory activity." Oh. He was right. We completed all the activities. *This week really has flown by*, I thought to myself. I tilted my head.

"You think I want to stop seeing you after last night?" I asked boldly. Caleb blushed fiercely and looked around, as if people could figure out that we fucked. "I'd like to do that again, if you feel the same," I said. Caleb continued blushing.

"I'd like that," he said shyly. This sent my heart hammering in my chest. *Oh, Caleb. What are you doing to me?*

"So, how are things going with Caleb?" Tracy asked. It was later that day, and Tracy had invited me to her house for some drinks. I thought about everything that had happened, the sex and everything else.

"Well...I might have kissed him again."

"What?!" Tracy shouted. I sighed. I should have expected this. She looked at me like I had four eyes.

"I thought you were going to *fix* things?" Tracy asked, shaking her head. "Not mess them up even more!"

I tapped my glass. "And... we might have gone further than just kissing," I admitted slowly.

Tracy's eyes were now bulging out of her head. She took a deep breath and a big swig of her drink. "You *defiled* Caleb Robinson?" she asked slowly. I smiled innocently.

Tracy punched me on the arm.

"Ow!" I said, rubbing my bicep. "What the fuck, Tracy?"

"You idiot! What about your movie? What if things go wrong? It'll fuck everything up!" she yelled.

I sighed. "The movie's gonna be just fine. Our chemistry on set should be amazing now, right? And things won't go wrong," I said. A nagging feeling poked me in the back, as if to say this wasn't true. I decided to ignore it.

Tracy looked at me in disbelief. "So, what, are you two like dating now? Or are you guys just fuck buddies?"

I looked down. "I'm…not entirely sure what we are. I just know that when I'm with him, I feel different. I don't feel as fucked up, or alone. I don't know how to describe it," I confessed.

Silence.

Tracy sighed and set her drink down. "Alright. But don't say I didn't warn you."

I was lost in my own thoughts. It's not like things could go *bad*, right?

What was the harm in a little fun?

CHAPTER 18

Caleb

The next day was Saturday and I was getting ready to go out and meet Lucy for lunch. I took a shower, got dressed and was about to head out when my phone buzzed. It was a text from…Brent. Shit. I'd forgotten about him.

Hey. U free to hang?

I stared at the text until my vision blurred. I didn't know what to say. I looked around the room, until my eyes landed on the sea turtle plush on the shelf. I suddenly knew the answer.

I can't today, sorry.

"How've things been going?" Lucy asked, taking a bite of her chopped salad.

I thought for a moment. *Should I tell Lucy about everything that's happened?* I'd feel guilty not telling her, since we basically told each other everything.

"There's…this guy," I started. Lucy focused all her attention on me.

"Go on," Lucy encouraged. I sighed.

"I'm not sure what we are. But we've been spending a lot of time together, and the more I get to know him, the more I think I like him," I confessed.

Lucy grinned from ear to ear. "That's amazing! Do I know him?" she asked.

I went silent for a moment. "It's…it's Remington. *Aaron* Remington."

Lucy didn't say anything at first. She stared at me, eyes crinkling in confusion. "*Moonlight Galaxy* Aaron?" she asked. I nodded hesitantly. Lucy leaned back in her chair. "That's…wow. I would've never guessed," she said.

I looked down. "I never expected it either. But I feel something when I'm with him. It's…different," I explained.

Lucy looked lost in thought. "And he feels the same?"

I thought about this. *Did* he feel the same? "I think so. I mean…I hope so," I said.

Lucy twirled her fork around. "I'm happy for you. I hope it works out for you guys. I just… don't want you to get hurt. Keeping a relationship under wraps, especially when you're a public figure is hard."

I nodded in agreement. She wasn't wrong. I knew there were a lot of risks involved. "I know that. But I think...I think it might be worth it," I declared.

Lucy smiled. "I'll be rooting for you, Caleb."

It would be worth it. Right?

On the way back, I saw I had a bunch of missed messages. My heart leapt to my throat. They were all from Brent. I scanned the messages, scrolling through.

Aw come on! I promise we'll have fun

Hello? U sure u can't come over?

Dude. Why r u ignoring me?

R u mad at me?

Can we please meet?

I sighed, my heart beating fast. Part of me felt bad for ignoring him, but the other part just wanted him to leave me alone. I slowly typed back, pondering on what to say. Finally, I typed out a message and hit *send.*

Hey. I didn't see ur texts until now. I'll come over.

Time to get this over with.

I pulled up to Brent's apartment. I didn't bother going through the back door this time. Brent opened the door, and I walked in.

"Dude, you're supposed to come through the back!" he shouted. I ignored him and just stood there. He looked at me in confusion. "Why were you not answering your texts?"

"Sorry. I had my phone on silent and was with a friend."

Brent slowly nodded. "Oh, alright. That's chill." He walked closer to me, tracing my arm with his fingers. I could smell alcohol on his breath. He leaned in to kiss me, but I looked away and took a step back. "Dude, what are you doing?" he asked.

I sighed. "I didn't come here for that," I explained.

Brent furrowed his brow. "Then why the hell are you here?" he asked.

I thought for a minute, trying to figure out how to put this into words. "I...don't think we should meet anymore," I finally said.

Brent scoffed. "Why not? Are you afraid of getting caught or something? Because I'm always careful and we make sure to always—"

I cut him off. "No, that's not why. I just don't think it's good for me to meet anymore. I just wanted to tell you in person."

Brent looked at me, obviously flabbergasted. "Is this…is this because I didn't want to be your *boyfriend*?" he finally asked in bewilderment. I looked away, not sure what to say. It wasn't about that, not really. I obviously couldn't tell him about Aaron. Brent took my silence as a yes and laughed nastily. "That's *rich*. Were you actually going into this expecting a relationship? That we'd get married and become Hollywood's gay 'it' couple?" he snickered. Anger welled inside me. Before I could stop myself, the words just came spilling out.

"You know what, Brent? That's actually *not* the reason why I don't want to meet anymore. The real reason is because you're a self-absorbed *asshole* who doesn't care about anyone's feelings but his own." I was shaking now. "And I don't need that in my life," I finished.

Brent blinked in surprise. He obviously wasn't used to being spoken to that way. I didn't bother to wait for him to respond, and I went to leave when he blocked the door. I glared at him.

"Get out of my way," I demanded. Brent just looked at me with those harsh green eyes.

"You shouldn't have said that," was all he said before stepping out of the way. I pushed past him and slammed the door shut on my way out.

I was panting as I got into my car. Well, that didn't go as expected. But it had to be done. Plus, it felt *good* getting rid of that negative energy. I always felt like shit after meeting with Brent, and there was no point in meeting anymore. I thought about Aaron and I smiled, feeling better.

Yeah, I definitely made the right decision.

CHAPTER 19

Aaron

"Can you explain it again?" Caleb asked for the hundredth time. I groaned.

"It's not that complicated," I said. It was Sunday and I invited Caleb over to watch the first *Moonlight Galaxy* movie. He turned to me, with those big blue eyes.

"I'm still confused!" he exclaimed.

I couldn't help but laugh. "Alright, fine. Basically, my character is a child with special powers. He thought he was just an orphan, but it turns out it's his destiny to fight against the main villain and save the galaxy from destruction," I said slowly so Caleb would understand.

He nodded as I spoke. "I still don't really understand the political jargon," he admitted.

I sighed. "No one does. If you know the gist of the story, you're good."

Caleb turned back to the screen. I could see him smiling from the corner of my eye.

"What?" I asked. He shook his head.

"It's interesting watching you as a child. You were so cute," he said. Then he blushed. "I-I mean, you still *are*," he stuttered. I grinned; he was so adorable. "How did you land this role?" Caleb asked.

I leaned back in the couch. "Honestly, I don't even know. My parents got me an agent through their connections, and I just started auditioning. The audition came up for this movie, which was expected to flop. I got the part, and the rest is history," I said.

Caleb stared at the screen, watching my younger self. "Wow," he said.

I shrugged. "It's because of my parents. It's not like I did anything."

Caleb shook his head in disagreement. "That's not true. I mean, yeah, you auditioned thanks to your parents' connections. But you were still chosen for the part and proved your talent. It's still because of your hard work," he insisted.

I was puzzled by Caleb's interpretations of my life, but it made me happy to hear. As the movie went on, I looked at Caleb who had his eyes closed. "Is it boring you?" I asked, smiling.

Caleb opened his eyes immediately. "No…well, maybe a little," he admitted, laughing.

I paused the movie and snickered. "Yeah, it's not for everyone," I said. I put my hand on Caleb's thigh, a mischievous glint in my eye. "Maybe I can do something to excite you?" I asked teasingly. Caleb blushed and I could feel his heartbeat quickening.

"I… I'd like that," he said. I slowly leaned in and pressed my mouth against his soft lips. As we kissed, I rubbed his leg, getting dangerously close to his cock. Caleb unbuttoned my shirt and caressed my chest, running his fingers through the dark hair gathered there. He kissed my neck and I groaned softly. He took off his shirt, then mine. He lowered himself to my chest and started lapping at my nipples, playing with the barbells. *Fuck.* I loved it when he did that.

I put my hands behind my head and closed my eyes, enjoying the sensation. He bit my nipples softly, twisting them with his tongue. I could feel him move on to my exposed armpits, licking and sucking at them while rubbing my nipples. Then, Caleb stood up and removed his pants and underwear. He was fully naked. He got on his knees in front of me and looked up. He had a sensual and submissive look in his eyes. It was a beautiful sight. If only Hollywood could see how their 'it' boy looked now. My cock twitched in anticipation. He pressed soft kisses to my lower abdomen and licked my happy trail. He unzipped my pants and lowered my underwear, my hard cock leaping out. Caleb wrapped his hand around my shaft and stroked it slowly, experimenting. I grunted and leaned back, savoring the moment.

"Your cock is beautiful," Caleb said.

I smiled at Caleb. "Not at beautiful as you," I retorted.

He shook his head as he continued stroking me. "I don't know. It's pretty fucking hot," he replied. My expression hardened and I decided to experiment a little.

"Enough talking. I want my cock in your pretty pink mouth. *Now,*" I ordered. I must have been doing something right, because I saw Caleb's cock twitch at this. He nodded obediently and wrapped his pink lips around my shaft, bobbing his head up and down.

"Slower, slower," I commanded. Caleb moved up and down slower, playing with my big balls in his other hand. He tongued the head of my dick, digging into the slit and licking around the shaft. I let this go on for a bit before I stood up. Caleb looked up at me in desperation and it was sight to see, with his mouth all red and saliva dripping down his chin.

"I wanna face-fuck you," I said, smacking my cock against Caleb's face a couple times. He nodded fast and put his mouth back on my cock. I grasped some of his hair with my hand and slowly started thrusting in and out of his mouth. Caleb wrapped his hands around my waist, clutching at my ass. I thrusted faster, encouraging him to deepthroat my dick.

"So fucking good. You're doing so fucking good, my little slut," I breathed out. I moved in and out, faster with each thrust as if I were fucking his little hole.

Eventually, I could feel my climax coming on, spreading from my thighs to my toes, about to explode.

"I'm gonna come in your mouth. I wanna see you swallow every last drop," I panted. The next few moments were a blur as I cried out and shot my load into Caleb's throat. He did a good job, swallowing it all in one swoop. I fell back onto the couch, recovering from my intense orgasm. I breathed heavily and Caleb came over and rested his head against my legs.

"Was I good?" he asked.

I grinned at Caleb, my eyes glazed over. "You were fucking amazing," I answered. Caleb seemed super happy to hear this and I squeezed his hand. "Is my verbal talk alright?" I asked. I didn't want to make Caleb upset or uncomfortable with my dominant nature. He kissed my hand.

"I fucking love it. I love verbal play, and you're amazing at it. Makes me so hard," he admitted.

I breathed out. "Good, I'm glad. If it's ever too much or you want to stop, just say the word," I assured him.

He nodded and looked at me sweetly. "Thank you."

"If you're still up for it, would you...want to have a little more fun?" I asked.

Caleb brightened. "Of course."

I led Caleb to my room and dug in my drawer. "You like poppers?" I asked him.

Caleb nodded. "I love them."

I grabbed a little bottle and inhaled it, letting myself become light headed. I tossed the bottle to Caleb who took a hit as well. We started making out, and I could feel my head begin to pound from the poppers. I breathed in.

"Wanna be inside me?" I asked. Caleb looked surprised.

"You want that?" he asked. I nodded. I really did. "Sure. I'd love to be inside you" he said. I took Caleb's hand and walked over to my bed.

"Lay down on your back," I said. He did as he was told, and I grabbed a condom from my bedside. I put it on Caleb and began to squat in front of him, lowering myself slowly on his hard cock. I could feel the blunt tip begin to enter my hole and I hissed. Finally, the entire head popped in and I cried out.

"Ah, fuck!" I yelled.

"Does it hurt?" Caleb asked, concerned.

I shook my head. "I can take it," I assured him. I lowered myself gently until his full length was inside me. Caleb groaned and closed his eyes.

"God, you're so fucking tight," he said. I raised my hips until just the tip was inside me and then slammed back down and Caleb yelped. I began bouncing on his cock, slowly at first. I felt so *full* and it felt so good. I stared bouncing up and down faster, breathing heavily. The poppers made me feel dizzy and my vision blurred at the edges, and I felt unreal. Caleb grabbed my hips and started thrusting up into me. *Fuck.* He kept pushing into me, fucking me like a jackhammer.

"Fuuuck," he cried out. I could feel his cock contract and I knew he was about to come.

"Come for me, sweetheart," I said. Caleb yelled and climaxed into me, the orgasm taking him over in waves. He panted heavily and lay there, with his eyes closed. I leaned down and kissed him softly on the lips.

"Good job," I whispered. I slowly lifted myself and pulled off his softening cock. Damn, I felt so empty afterwards. I lay next to Caleb, who was still recovering. I kissed his cheek and cuddled into him. "Feel good?" I asked.

His eyes widened. "I usually don't top, but being inside you felt fucking *incredible*," he said. I wrapped my arms around him and he wrapped his arms around me, both of us naked and sweaty, the smell of cum and sex in the air. We fell asleep like this, our limbs tangled together as one.

The next morning, Caleb and I took a shower together. I rinsed him off, washing his back and admiring his ass. He washed my back and legs, and Caleb might have given me another blowjob. *Might* have. Afterwards, I walked him out. It was cold outside, so I put on a hoodie and followed him to his car. Caleb turned to me.

"I had an amazing time," he said. I looked around to make sure no one was around and leaned in to kiss Caleb goodbye. Caleb closed his eyes and kissed me back gently, our tongues gliding together. We pulled apart and Caleb got into his car and drove off, waving goodbye. I made my way back into the house, and turned around, watching Caleb drive away. I smiled wistfully, already wanting him to come back.

CHAPTER 20

Caleb

The following Monday, Aaron called me. "You free? I want to take you out somewhere," he said over the phone. I smiled to myself.

"Aaron Remington, are you asking me out on a *date?*" I asked in amazement.

He snickered. "Maybe I am," he replied.

I pretended to think about it. "Hmm…alright, fine. Where are we going?" I asked.

"It's a surprise," Aaron answered. I pouted to myself. "I'll pick you up. Dress light," he said.

"Sounds good," I replied before hanging up. I couldn't help but grin. Technically, Aaron and I had been on dates, if you counted the mandatory activities, but this was the first time he asked me out on an actual date. I was excited and I didn't even know where we were going. He said to dress light, so I picked out a blue tank top, shorts, and of course a baseball cap and dark sunglasses. About twenty minutes later, I heard a car honk out front, and I went outside to see Aaron in his red mustang. I smiled like a fool and got into his car. Aaron was also wearing a hat and dark sunglasses, along with a tank top, showing off his muscular biceps. He looked deliciously hot. He looked at me and grinned.

"Hey, sexy," he said. My heart fluttered and I put my seatbelt on.

"So, where are we off to?" I asked.

Aaron turned on the radio and started driving. "You'll see," he said.

I felt so free, riding in this car with Aaron, the cold wind hitting my face. It felt like a dream. We rode through the streets of Santa Monica, radio blasting. Eventually, I saw the familiar sight of the pier. I gasped with excitement.

"Are we going to the beach?" I asked like a child. Aaron shrugged like it was no big deal, his arm hanging out the window. Aaron found parking and we got out of the car. I breathed in the salty, fresh air, letting the sun hit my face. Aaron held out his hand and I took it. It should be fine, right? No one would probably recognize us with our hats and sunglasses. We just looked like two normal dudes holding hands. We walked along the boardwalk, and I could see the giant Ferris wheel towering above.

"What do you wanna do?" Aaron asked. I thought about it and looked around as we walked. Then I spotted a merry-go-round. I grinned and pulled Aaron along, breaking into a run. I stopped in front of the merry-go-round and Aaron just looked at me over his sunglasses.

"Seriously?" he asked.

I gave him my best puppy dog eyes. "Pleaaase?" I asked. Aaron sighed.

"Alright, but only because I can't resist those eyes." I grinned and we got on the ride. I chose a white horse that was bedazzled with jewels and Aaron chose a black horse with gold accents. Eventually, the ride started, and we must have looked like two fools, but I didn't care. I was *happy*. I reached out my hand to Aaron, who took it and squeezed. As we got off, I looked at Aaron.

"How are you doing?" I asked. Aaron shook his head.

"Dizzy, now." I laughed and we went off to ride the Ferris wheel next. We climbed in and were right up on each other due to us both being grown men. But I didn't mind, and I don't think Aaron did either. We made it to the top and the wheel stopped there for a moment. I looked out, admiring the beautiful view of the ocean and the sun. It was breathtaking. I looked at Aaron, who was staring at me as if *I* were the breathtaking view. He kissed the side of my head, and I rested my head against his shoulder, holding on to his bicep. I felt like my heart was going to burst out of my chest. I never wanted this moment to end. I would cherish this memory, always. The wheel started making its way down and we got off.

"Now what?" I asked. Aaron looked around, spotting a food cart.

"Want some ice cream?" he asked. We each got a cone and walked hand in hand. I'd always wanted to go on a date like this. I never thought it would be possible for me. We explored some of the shops, and I noticed a necklace with a sea turtle pendant hanging off it. I bought it when Aaron wasn't looking, and I handed it to him. He looked at me, perplexed.

"What's this?" he asked. I shrugged and he rummaged through the bag. He stared at the pendant, smiling.

"A sea turtle," he said.

I nodded. "Just like the one you gave me." Aaron put it on around his neck.

"I love it," he said. My insides flipped and I took a lick of my ice cream cone. We were walking along the boardwalk, and I stopped for a moment, looking out at the sunset. The hues of pink, orange, and yellow blurred together and reflected off the ocean waves. It was a sight to behold. I was so mesmerized by it that I almost didn't hear the yelling.

"Oh my God, is that Caleb Robinson?!" a girl shrieked.

My heart stopped. *Oh no. Not here.* A group of girls came running up to us and Aaron took a few steps backward from me.

"Oh my God, you *are* Caleb Robinson! I love all your movies!" one of the girls yelled. I smiled politely, although inside I was freaking out. Had they seen us holding hands together? Did they *know*?

"Thank you," I said.

"Can we get a picture?" another girl asked.

"Of course," I said automatically. I looked at Aaron apologetically and he got the cue. He took one of the girls' phones and snapped a picture of us.

"Thank you so much!" the girls yelled and ran off, giggling. My heart hammered in my chest and I just stood there in shock.

"Hey," Aaron said, touching my arm. I instinctively pulled away and I instantly regretted it. Aaron looked hurt, and I felt horrible.

"Sorry," I said. "It's just…" I looked away in pain.

Aaron nodded. "It's ok. I understand," he said. We walked silently back to the car and he drove me back to my place. We didn't talk during the drive, and I wanted to cry. How could such a perfect day get ruined like that? *Why* did I have to get recognized? As Aaron stopped at my driveway, I looked at him.

"I'm sorry. I just…was scared," I admitted.

Aaron nodded. "I know. I'm sorry too, for putting you in that position," he said.

My eyes widened. "No, Aaron, it's absolutely not your fault. You…you gave me an incredible gift. A memory I'll never forget. I really…" I opened my mouth and then shut it. What was I trying to say? I sighed and looked down. I couldn't get my thoughts together. Aaron didn't say anything as I got out of the car. I slowly started walking and I turned to say *thank you* for today, but Aaron was already gone. Tears blurred the corners of my eyes.

Why did this have to be so fucking hard?

CHAPTER 21

Aaron

I drove off, feeling confused and guilty. I arrived at my house and collapsed on my bed. As I stared at the ceiling, I thought about the day's events. It had started off so *well.* I thought about the way Caleb got excited to go on the merry-go-round like a child, the way he snuggled against me in the Ferris wheel. I thought about the way the sunset reflected off his face, casting a golden hue around him. I touched the turtle pendant around my neck. No one has ever really given me a gift like that before. I thought about Caleb and his happy smile as we ate ice cream. I wanted to make sure that Caleb *always* had a smile like that. Then, I thought about Caleb's face as those group of girls came up to him. He looked *terrified.* I didn't blame him; I would've been scared too. I knew what he was thinking: *had they seen us together? Was our secret out?* I blamed myself. I should've known better than to have put Caleb in that situation. I didn't want to jeopardize his career or ruin his reputation. That was the *last* thing I wanted. If we were discovered and it hurt Caleb, I would never be able to forgive myself. I sighed and rubbed my hands over my face.

Why did this have to be so complicated? Not only was our relationship risky, but there was also a nagging thought in the back of my mind: that I wasn't good enough for Caleb, that I would only be a detriment to him. After all, all I did was fuck everything up. Caleb deserved more than that; he deserved someone who could promise him a future. *Could I do that?* I wasn't sure. I didn't even know what *my* future looked like, let alone ours. I thought about what Tracy said before, about her warning. Was she right? *Was* it too risky? Maybe I should reach out to her and ask for some advice. I didn't really have anyone else to turn to at this point. I thought about my sister. If only we still had a good relationship, I could have asked her for advice. Or if I had parents who actually *cared* about my problems. God, I was pathetic. I couldn't stand being alone anymore, so I decided to give Tracy a call. Maybe she would have some insight.

A little while later, Tracy came over for drinks. She stirred her margarita, lost in thought.

"I see. You guys were almost caught," she said. I nodded.

"Yeah, and Caleb looked horrified when his fans came up to him," I said, wincing as I thought about it.

"Did you guys talk about it?" she asked. I shook my head.

"Not really. I felt guilty so I apologized but he seemed shaken up."

Tracy was quiet for a moment. "It's a hard situation."

"I just don't want to hurt him or hurt his career. I'd be so upset with myself if that happened," I said.

Tracy sipped her drink, her dark hair falling over her shoulders. "You might not be able to control that," she said. She looked at me seriously. "You guys need to decide if this is something serious or just a fleeting moment of fun. Because if you don't take it seriously, you both could end up hurt," she said. She looked down. "If this *is* something serious, you both must be prepared for the consequences. You guys can't hide forever. If you really *do* love him, you have to be prepared to potentially let him go if you think it will hurt his career," she said.

My heart jumped at the word *love*. Was that what this was? *Love?* Was I in *love* with Caleb Robinson? I haven't known him for very long. Could people fall in love that quickly? I wasn't sure.

"Although, I'm just a hypocrite," Tracy shrugged. "After all, I'm hiding my own relationship."

I was silent for a moment, feeling sympathy for Tracy. "I'm sorry. I never realized how hard you have it," I said.

Tracy shrugged like it was no big deal. "It is what it is," she replied. I sat there, lost in thought.

"Do you…think I should break things off?" I asked hesitantly.

Tracy sighed and leaned back. "I really don't know. I mean, if you guys come out publicly, it will impact his career in a lot of different ways. If he's not ready to come out, it might be better to end it now rather than later," she advised. I went silent. I didn't *want* to break things off. But if it was better for Caleb and his life, then I would do anything to make him happy. *If you really love something, you have to set it free.* That was a saying, right? Maybe it was true in this scenario. I sighed, leaning back in my chair.

This fucking sucked.

CHAPTER 22

Caleb

The Monday afternoon was turning into the evening, and Aaron still hadn't texted me.

Was he mad at me? I wondered. I lay on my bed, hugging the sea turtle plush. I couldn't think of a reason *why* he'd be mad. If anything, he seemed to think *he* was in the wrong. I breathed out and looked at the turtle.

"What do you think I should do?" I asked aloud, staring into its beaded eyes. It stared back at me, offering no advice. I sighed. "Yeah, that's what I thought." I could feel myself about to drift off into sleep, when my phone buzzed. I glanced at it and my heart stopped. *Aaron.*

Hey. Could I come over?

I quickly typed back.

Yes, come over. I'll be here.

My spirits rose a little. Aaron *wasn't* upset with me. That was good at least. Maybe we could fix things, talk things through. I started feeling hopeful and I got up, putting Remy back on the shelf. I made sure I looked alright and ate a sandwich while I waited for him to arrive. Finally, from the window I saw his familiar red mustang pull up. I rose from the table and opened the door, inviting him in. He smiled at me, but it didn't seem genuine.

"Hi," I said. He looked at me, and there was something sad in his eyes. My heart hammered in my chest. Was he alright?

"Hi," he said back. Some silence.

"Do you...want to sit down?" I asked, gesturing to the couch. He shook his head.

"No, no...I won't be too long," he explained. My stomach dropped. This was already heading in a bad direction. Why did this feel so *awkward*? He swallowed, and I watched his Adam's apple move up and down.

"When you...when you love something, you have to set it free," he stated, as if reciting a speech. I just stood there, in complete and utter shock. I couldn't even comprehend the entire phrase. All I heard was the word *love*. Did Aaron just say he *loved* me? A part of me felt happiness, but the other part knew something was wrong. I didn't know what to say. Aaron continued. "Caleb...I've been doing a lot of thinking," he said. *Oh no.* That wasn't a good start. He paced the floor. "It's funny. When I met you—*before* I even met you—I thought you were some goody-two shoes. That we could never get along," he paused. "But the more I got to know you, I realized…I was wrong. That you are an amazing and kindhearted person." Aaron breathed out. "I don't want you to suffer or hurt because of me. I want you to be happy and have an amazing, long career. I don't want you to have to sneak around or hide from the world. You deserve better than that," he insisted. I realized what this was. This was a *break-up* speech.

"Aaron," I started. He cut me off, holding up his hand.

"Just let me finish," he pleaded. I shut my mouth and nodded. "I'm not… a good person. I'm selfish and can be a major asshole," he admitted. "You deserve someone better. Which is why I'm ending things." Tears blurred my vision, and I just shook my head in disbelief. Was he *serious*? I could see tears glisten in Aaron's eyes too. "I'm sorry," he croaked out. Anger welled up inside me.

"No. *No.* You don't get to do that," I said, shaking. "You don't get to…to waltz into my life and make me feel things I've never felt before with *anybody*. You don't get to make me fall madly in *love* with you and then just…take it all away!" I shouted in grief. Aaron just stared at me in shock. And then he shook his head.

"Caleb. I need you to think. Are you able to come out publicly? Are you *able* to do that and be alright when everything changes? When the hurricane hits?" he asked. I opened my mouth to say that, of course I was, but then shut it. Was I okay with that? *Was* I ready to come out to the world? I... I didn't know. Aaron nodded sadly.

"I would never want to hurt you or pressure you to do anything. Which is why I'm *doing* this," he iterated. Tears streamed down my face, but I didn't care.

"You don't get to make that decision!" I cried out.

Aaron turned to leave. "I'm sorry, Caleb. I really am. Trust me, you'll have dodged a bullet. You might not realize it now, but you will," he said. Then he walked out the door.

"Aaron!" I shouted, running after him. I ran to his car, and I collapsed, falling to my knees. "Please don't leave! I... I *love* you!" I shouted. Aaron looked at me, tears glittering in his eyes.

And then he drove off. I just sat there on the pavement, crying.

What the fuck just happened?

I spent the next couple of hours crying in my room. I really only had myself to blame. It was because of *me* we couldn't be together. It was because of *me* we had to keep quiet. My dreams had come true, but at what cost? Was it worth it if I was so miserable? I stared at the framed photo on my dresser. It was a picture of me with my parents and siblings. I started crying even more because *now* I felt homesick. Fuck, I was a crybaby. Home was only about an hour and a half away. Maybe it would do me some good to hang out with my family.

I slowly got up from my bed and went to the bathroom to wash my face. I had pretty much cried myself out. My eyes were red and puffy and I looked like a mess. I tried my best to fix my appearance before heading out. When I pulled up to my parents' home, I trudged out of my car and rang the doorbell. My sister opened the door. She looked at me, surprised.

"What are you doing here?" she asked.

I shrugged and stepped inside. "I was feeling homesick," I admitted and looked around. "Are mom and dad home?" I asked, noticing that it was quiet.

Sofia shook her head. "Nah, they went out on a date. So I've just been here alone."

I nodded slowly. "Oh, ok." We sat on the couch, and she got us some sodas from the fridge. Mittens leaped onto my lap, and I scratched her ear absent-mindedly.

"It's actually good you're here. I've been bored as hell," Sofia said. I laughed a little. Sofia got bored easily. But then again, so did I. I sighed and took a sip of soda. Sofia peered closer at me, inspecting me. "You've been crying," she observed. I shut my eyes. *Of course* she could tell I had been crying. My eyes were probably still red.

"Homesick," I explained. Well, partially explained.

Sofia raised an eyebrow. "Is that all?"

I nodded and then shook my head, the tears starting to come back. *God damn it.* I sniffed and looked at her. "There's a guy," I said.

Sofia nodded knowingly. "Yeah, that's usually how it starts," she said.

I was silent for a moment. "He...I thought he was an ass at first. But the more I got to know him, I started really liking him." Sofia nodded, waiting for me to go on. "It's just...everything's been so complicated since I became famous," I admitted. "I thought my dreams coming true would make me happy, but I just feel awful. We have to sneak around and I can't tell the world about our relationship. I'm *scared*," I said. "What if the world doesn't accept me? What if they decide they don't like me anymore?"

Sofia sighed and looked away. "Aaron...you can't control if people like you or what others think. You can only control what *you* think about yourself." I nodded along. She was right about that. "I'm happy that your dream came true, I really am," she continued. "I do worry about you sometimes, though. I can tell you're not always completely happy. You have to ask yourself if your dream is *worth* the cost. And you have to ask yourself, what if the world truly saw who Caleb Robinson was?" Sofia looked at me. "And you have a point. There's always a possibility the world will reject us, or not like us. But we have to show ourselves anyway. Even if we're rejected. Because in the end, only *you* can accept yourself." She paused. "And, if for some reason things did go to shit, you always have a place here with us."

I smiled, grateful for her words. Sofia was surprisingly mature for her age. I hugged her, and she squirmed, pushing me away. "I love you," I said.

She rolled her eyes. "Yeah, yeah," she said back. She punched me in the arm playfully. "So. Did you get me Henry Cavill's autograph yet?" she asked jokingly.

I burst out laughing. "Sofia, I met him once, and he didn't even know who I was!" I exclaimed. "Plus, I was too nervous. The man is *fucking hot*!" I shouted.

Sofia laughed along. "You got a point there." We chatted a bit more before it was time for me to head out. I was right to go home. Talking with Sofia made me feel a lot better. I was grateful to have my family. Maybe things would work themselves out. It couldn't get any worse, *right*?

CHAPTER 23

Aaron

It was now late at night on that same Monday. I took a drag of my cigarette and slowly exhaled. I had done it. I had broken things off with Caleb. It was a lot harder than I thought it would be. All I could think about is Caleb crying out on the driveway, saying that he loved me. I felt like a monster for leaving him there. But what could I do? Caleb might not see it now, but he'll realize soon enough that he's too good for me. I had done the right thing. Now Caleb's career would be safe, and he wouldn't have me weighing him down. I wasn't sure what would happen with the movie now. Caleb probably wouldn't want to work with me anymore, and I didn't blame him. I guess I'd have to find an actual job, now that the movie was out of the question.

Fuck. I twirled the turtle necklace, and I didn't want to take it off, but there was no point in wearing it now. I unclasped the necklace and tucked it away in the compartment behind the *Moonlight Galaxy* poster. Just another thing to add to my list of failures. I went to take a shower, which just reminded me of Caleb, which made me think of Caleb *naked. Fuck.* I started to get hard at the thought. Even when he wasn't here, he was turning me on. I tried to get him out of my mind, but I thought of him naked and on the floor, his lips all red and swollen. Saliva dripping down his chin. I was fully erect now and I knew it wouldn't go away. I grasped my erection and slowly started stroking as the water ran down my body. I closed my eyes and thought of face-fucking Caleb, his cheeks full as he deepthroated my cock. I thought about Caleb and his sweet round ass, the way his hole gripped my dick tightly. I breathed harder and could feel myself getting close. Finally, I thought of Caleb and his sweet smile, the way he looked when he saw the sunset. That threw me over the edge. I cried out and my cock spurted jets of cum out onto the shower floor. I panted heavily and collected myself, gripping the wall.

Fuck. *What was happening to me?*

"So… you broke it off?" Tracy asked tentatively. I slowly nodded as I sipped my drink. It was now Tuesday morning and I was out having drinks with Tracy at a nearby restaurant.

"Yeah. It's done," I confirmed.

Tracy looked at me with sympathy. "How do you feel?"

I sighed and leaned back. "Like shit," I admitted. "I did it because I wanted the best for Caleb. I didn't want to be a burden to him or his career," I explained. "But I still feel like shit," I said, shaking my head.

Tracy nodded, stirring her drink. "I think that's normal. You really liked him, I could tell. I've never seen you get serious about someone like that before."

I shrugged. "I never thought there was someone out there who would accept me," I said. "But he did. He didn't care that I was fucked up, or that I hurt people in the past. He still loved me anyway." I sniffed and looked away. *No.* I was not gonna cry. Not here.

Tracy exhaled. "How did he take it?" she asked.

I thought again about Caleb on the pavement, crying. "Not well," I just said. I took a swig of my drink and slammed it down. "He'll realize though. Maybe not now, but he will. He'll realize that I did this *because* I love him," I said. *Who was I trying to convince?* I wasn't sure.

Tracy lowered her eyes. "Maybe, when Caleb figures things out, you guys can try again," she said hesitantly.

I shook my head. "No. He deserves someone better than me. I'm too…sullied," I said.

Tracy gave me a look. "You're not *sullied*. You're just jaded," she said.

I laughed and shrugged. "Maybe," I replied. "How's Sasha?" I'd been so busy with own relationship drama I didn't ask Tracy about her own.

Tracy lit up. "She's good! We went on a date recently. It was nice," she said.

I hesitated. "How do you guys deal with it? Does she ever get upset that the world thinks you're dating me?" I asked.

Tracy looked down. "Sometimes. She gets upset about it at times, and I'm constantly wondering if I should break up with her to spare her feelings. But I don't know. It's complicated," she said. "Here, I'll show you a photo of her dog," Tracy said, scrolling through her phone. Then her expression changed. She covered her mouth with her hand and her eyes went wide. "*Fucking shit*," she cried out.

"What? What is it?" I pressed. Tracy slowly lowered her hand and swallowed.

"It's...you should read it for yourself," she said, handing me the phone. I looked at her, confused and slowly took the phone. I scanned the screen and my heart dropped. I felt like I was going to vomit.

Caleb Robinson has a secret gay lover?!

"This morning, paparazzi recently made photos public of what appears to be up-and-coming movie star, Caleb Robinson, sharing an intimate moment with an unknown man. Robinson is known for his leading roles in numerous romance movies, such as *The Bleeding Rose*. Although Robinson has never commented on his sexuality, the rising star hasn't publicly come out as gay. This is sure to break the hearts of his fans, many of whom are teenage girls…"

I didn't bother to read the rest of the article. I stared at an image of Caleb kissing me in front of my house. His face was in full view, but my back was turned with my hoodie up. The photo seemed to have been taken from behind the bushes.

No. Fucking. Way.

I excused myself to the bathroom, with Tracy calling after me. I locked myself in a stall, breathing heavily. Only one thought rang in my head: *This was all my fault.*

CHAPTER 24

Caleb

Buzz, Buzz, Buzz...

I groaned, turning over in my bed. I was still half-asleep, and I didn't want to look at my phone right now. I breathed softly and closed my eyes when...

Buzz, Buzz, Buzz...

Ugh. Who kept trying to call me? I sighed heavily and forced myself to get up. I grabbed my phone from the dresser and frowned. My phone was flooded with messages. My sister Sofia, my old costar Alison, my agent, my manager, and Lucy. That was strange.

I tapped on the first message, which was Alison's.

Caleb, I'm so sorry!! I swear I had nothing to do with it!!

My heart froze. What the hell was she talking about? I tapped Sofia's message:

Caleb, I can't fucking believe they would do that. Call me as soon as you can, alright? Please hang in there. I love you!

My breathing got faster. Something was seriously wrong. I tapped Lucy's message.

Caleb!! Are u ok?! I heard the news! Please call me! I'm worried about you!

Why was everyone being so cryptic?! What the fuck was going on?!

I finally clicked my agent's message.

Call me ASAP. We need to discuss how we're going to handle this.

There was an attachment to a tabloid. I clicked on it, and an article came up. As I read it, I felt like the world was falling apart. My breath froze and I thought I was gonna throw up. My cheeks went hot, and my heartbeat raced dangerously fast. I dropped the phone and went to vomit in the toilet. I lay there on the bathroom floor, not quite believing what I had just read.

It was official. The world knew. And I didn't even get to have a choice in the matter.

After the shock and nausea wore off, anger kicked in. The fucking paparazzi. What the fuck was their problem? Were they *stalking* me now? This was supposed to be *my* choice. *My* decision to tell who and where and when. Now it was all ruined.

I should have been more careful. I shouldn't have kissed Aaron in public like that, or even held hands. *What the fuck was wrong with me?* I started to cry, tears filling my eyes. I cried on the floor, tasting vomit in my mouth. Then I thought about Aaron. *Did…he have something to do with the leak? No. No. He would never do that.* I hated myself for even considering that. I picked up my phone and looked at the picture again. It was clearly me, but Aaron's back was turned. I threw my phone on the floor. Everything had officially gone to shit. People wouldn't look at me the same now. I'd always be that one 'gay actor' and that's all I'd be known as. That's all people would see in me. I didn't want to check the articles comments or my social media, but I couldn't help myself. As I scanned the comments, I was a little relieved to see that most were supportive. People were bashing the paparazzi for leaking the photo. People were making comments such as:

> *The paparazzi is so invasive! Caleb should come out when he's ready!*
>
> *Paparazzi are fucking gross. Poor Caleb, I hope he's alright!*
>
> *I support Caleb! I don't care if he's gay, I'll always be a fan!*

Who cares if he's gay? That's his own business! Leave the man alone!

There's nothing wrong with being gay. Fuck the paparazzi!

I agreed with these comments, and they made me feel a little better. Of course, there were some negative comments as well.

Well, I'm officially not watching his movies anymore.

I knew there was something off about him! No one can be that perfect.

Gross. And to think I had a crush on this dude.

God doesn't approve. I hope he turns to religion.

Fucking faggot.

I'd be lying if I said these didn't make me feel like shit, especially the last one. But they did. And it *hurt*.

There were also some comments along the lines of, *Fuck! All the hot guys are always gay! Now I'll never have a chance with him!*

Those comments made me smile a little. Luckily, the supportive comments outweighed the negative by a lot. But still, the little negativity got to me. The fact that some people would stop being a fan simply because I liked the same gender wa*s appalling* to me. I sniffed, and slowly got up from the floor. I looked in the mirror at my reflection. My eyes were red and there was some vomit on the corner of my mouth. My hair was sticking up, and my cheeks were completely wet. I looked *fucking horrific.* I took a deep breath, trying to calm myself. I needed to shower.

I wondered what my life would be like now. *Would people treat me differently? Would I get turned down for certain roles now?* Then I started wondering if maybe this would *help* people. Help other queer people who didn't have someone to look up to, to relate to. I pondered this. Maybe some good *would* come out of this, after all. My thoughts turned to Aaron. I noticed he hadn't texted me. Why would he? He shut me out. I wondered what he thought of all this. He was probably relieved no one knew it was him. I was glad for that; I didn't want Aaron to be burdened by this too.

I got out of the shower and dried off, then got dressed. *Should I even go outside today?* I wasn't sure. I should probably call back my agent and let everyone know I was still alive. But the only person I really wanted to talk was Aaron. I knew that wasn't possible; he broke up with me. I went to call my agent when I heard a knock at the door, and there was...Aaron. He was standing there, in a red flannel and black jeans, looking at me with those dark eyes.

"Hey," he said. I shook my head in confusion.

"What are *you* doing here?" I asked in anger.

He sighed. "I know you're mad at me, and for good reason. But I just *had* to make sure you were ok."

I looked down at his shoes. "You heard," I said.

He nodded. "Yeah. Yeah, I heard. And Caleb…I know this won't fix things but I am *so* fucking sorry. This is all my fault and I know I can't undo what's happened. I just wanted you to know that I'm sorry." He released his breath.

I nodded slowly. "It's fine. It's not your fault. Really, it was my own for being so careless."

Aaron rubbed his face with his hands. "This is why I broke things off. Because I fuck everything up. I fuck people over and everyone who gets close to me gets hurt," he bemoaned.

I shook my head in anger. "That isn't true. I've told you this. I know you won't believe me, but I don't think you're a fuck-up."

I looked at him, pleading in my eyes. *Come back to me*, they said. Aaron seemed to read this, but he just stepped backwards. "It's better if you stay away from me," he said before running off to his car and driving away. I just stood there, feeling déjà vu. I exhaled shakily and went back inside. I looked around and stared at Remy the turtle, who stared back mockingly. Tears welled in my eyes, but I didn't allow them to be fully released. *Why did it have to come to this?*

"We've prepared a public statement from you." This was the first thing my agent said to me as I walked into her office. I sat down and tentatively took the paper, reading the statement.

Dear fans,

I wanted to release a statement regarding the recent photos leaked of me. First off, I wanted to apologize for hiding and keeping you all in the dark. It was not my intention to lie or mislead you. The truth is, I will be starring in an upcoming queer romance film and that man in the photo is only my co-star. I am so sorry to confuse you all. Secondly, I wanted to thank you for all your love and support during this time. You all are the reason for my success. Please keep supporting me and I'll keep trying to do my best!

—Caleb Robinson

I frowned, staring at the paper. Anger made its way inside me. They wanted me to *deny* it? Fuck. That. I tore the paper in half, and my agent gaped at me.

"No. I'm not releasing this statement," I said firmly. My agent then sighed and sat down.

"Caleb, your publicity team and I have discussed this and we really think it's best if—"

I cut her off. "I'm not *denying* it. I'm not ashamed of who I am. If I lose fans because of this, that's on *them*. They weren't really my fans to begin with. I'm not apologizing, either. I should have gotten to decide when to come out, not be fucking *shoved* out of the closet." I breathed heavily, shaking with anger.

My agent was silent. "So…do you want to make this an official coming out statement?" she asked.

I sighed in frustration. "Why do I need to make a statement at all? This is my own fucking personal life! Who I sleep with is no one's business but my own! I shouldn't have to make an announcement to the whole fucking world!" I stood up in rage.

My agent rested her hands on the desk. "Calm down, Caleb. We're only trying to *help* you. You're right; this is your personal life. It should be no one's business but your own. But the truth of the matter is, you're a public figure now. You don't have a personal life anymore, not really. That's how it is for celebrities. The burden of fame. So, like it or not, you really *do* need to make a public statement about this. Whether that's denying it or coming out is up to you," she said.

I took a breath and sat back down. "Fine. I'll make a statement. But it'll be my *own* words and the truth," I said, no room for negotiation. My expression hardened.

"I'm not hiding or running away. Not anymore."

CHAPTER 25

Aaron

I took a drag of my cigarette and stared at my crumpled article and turtle necklace. I was in my shame room, looking at my failures. I don't know what the fuck was wrong with me. I was officially back to square one. I blew out some smoke and shook my head. I really was a pathetic fuck-up. Not only did I fuck my family over, now I've fucked Caleb over, the *one* person I didn't want to hurt. *Why did it always turn out this way for me?* I thought about meeting Caleb at the shoot. I thought he would have a boring personality and be your typical perfect 'it' boy. A stick-in-the-mud. But he ended up being so much more than that, so many layers to him and I didn't even get to see them all. I thought about meeting that first day at the bowling alley; he obviously didn't want to be there, and neither did I. I thought of our day at the aquarium, how he got excited over little things and didn't care that I was afraid of sharks. The arcade, where I kissed him. Running to find him at the karaoke bar. Singing together, having a picnic together. Having sex. Visiting the beach and riding the Ferris wheel. All of it. I loved every single moment. And now, none of it even *mattered*. All of it amounted to nothing, and Caleb had to pay the price.

I closed my eyes, head throbbing. It wasn't *fair*. I sighed and put out my cigarette. I pulled out my phone, staring again at the invasive photo. Anger pulsed through me. What the fuck was the paparazzi even doing at my house? It made no sense. The paparazzi didn't care about me, not anymore. Obviously, they were there somehow and it fucking *sucked*. I looked at my contacts, trying to see if there was anyone to talk to. There was Tracy, but I've already bothered her enough with this crap. I hovered my finger over my sister's number. A longing passed through me. The truth was I *missed* my sister. I missed hanging out with her, watching movies and complaining about our parents. *Was it too late to fix our relationship?* I knew she wasn't a fan of me, and I didn't blame her. From her perspective, I was just a greedy asshole. Which was true, for the most part. I pressed her name and listened to the dial tone. After a few moments, she picked up.

"What do you want?" she asked, already annoyed.

"Hey…are you busy?"

"Well, I was hanging with Jonah." Jonah was Megan's longtime boyfriend.

"Do you need something? Is this about money? Because if it is, I'm not—" I cut her off.

"It's not about money. I just…felt lost. And I needed to talk to someone," I confessed.

There was some silence. "Alright," she said cautiously, waiting for me to go on.

I thought about what I wanted to say and gathered my words. "Look. I know that you haven't liked me for a long time, and I don't blame you. I didn't like me either. I was—*am*—selfish and unreliable, and I can understand why you cut ties with me. I just wanted to…apologize. For everything. For not being there when you needed me and for only thinking of myself." I paused for a moment and Megan didn't say anything, so I kept going. "I recently…met someone. And they taught me a lot of things about myself. And the truth is, I miss you. I really do want to try and rekindle our relationship, if that's something you want," I said nervously.

There was a long silence. I wondered for a moment if Megan left or if she hung up. Finally, she spoke. "Thank you…for the apology. I…can't promise that our relationship will be the same as it was. But if you really have reflected and changed, then…I'm willing to at least try," she said. I breathed out. She continued. "I'm also glad that you met someone. Do I know her?" she asked.

I hesitated. I guess there was no beating around the bush this time. "Actually…that's another thing. I've never told you this, or mom and dad. And I don't know if I will tell them right now. The fact is, I'm bisexual. The person I met is a guy."

Megan cleared her throat. "Wow, Aaron. Why didn't you ever tell me? Back when we were on speaking terms? I would've accepted it, you know."

I shrugged even though Megan couldn't see. "I don't know. I guess I didn't want to burden anyone. I already did that enough," I said.

"Well...I'm glad you told me. And I'm glad you met that guy. I hope things work out for you both," Megan replied.

My heart sunk a little. "Actually...things didn't end up working out. It doesn't diminish what he taught me, but it's over," I said sadly.

A pause. "Huh. That's interesting," she said.

I frowned. "What is?" I asked.

"It's not like you to just give up on something like that. Usually, you're more stubborn. You always try to get what you want," she said.

I thought about this. That *was* true, usually. But this time was different. "I had to let him go. It was better for him," I explained, trying to convince her. Or was I trying to convince myself? I didn't know anymore.

"Well, I hope you made the right decision," Megan said.

When we ended the call I felt…lighter. Less depressed. At least I was able to rekindle one relationship. Her words rang in my head. *It's not like you to just give up on something.* Was that what this was? Was I giving up on him? Or was I giving up on *myself?*

CHAPTER 26

Caleb

I decided to visit my family later that day. I figured I should let them at least know I was still alive and breathing. I got on the freeway and pulled up to my parent's house. I rang the bell, and my mom opened the door. She looked at me with sympathy and sighed.

"Oh, honey," she said, shaking her head. She pulled me into a hug, and it felt *good*. She pulled back and invited me in. "Come sit," she said, patting the couch, where Mittens was sleeping.

"Where's dad?" I asked.

"Oh, he's at work. Your sister's home though, I think she's upstairs."

I nodded, looking around. "So… I'm guessing you saw the news?" I asked grimly.

She nodded, concern in her eyes. "I saw. And it made me so *angry*. That's a total invasion of privacy!"

I smiled, but it didn't reach my eyes. "Yeah, well. The paparazzi don't exactly care about privacy."

My mom took my hand. "I'm so sorry. I know you didn't want the world to know yet. I can't understand how you must be feeling, but I'm always here for you." I nodded, thankful for my mom's support. She paused. "So...do you want to tell me anything?" she asked hesitantly. I was confused as to what she was referring to, then I slowly realized.

"Oh...you want to know about the guy?" I asked.

She nodded. "If you want to talk about it. You don't have to," she said.

I exhaled and looked away out the window. "There *was* a guy. But...it's over now," I explained. It hurt me to say this out loud.

"Do you want to talk about it?" she asked. "It makes me sad to see you upset."

I didn't know if I wanted to talk about it right now. But maybe it would help me see things differently, putting it into words. "We met through a film shoot, and we didn't like each other at first. But we got to know each other, and before I knew it I... fell in love," I admitted. "But, because of my secret and his own issues...it became complicated. He broke things off, thinking it would be best for me," I said, getting angry again. "How does *he* know what's best for me? I should be able to make my own decisions, but it seems like everyone wants to make them for me!" I shouted angrily.

My mom looked at me and thought for a moment. "That must be very frustrating," she agreed. "I think that, sometimes, when someone loves you a lot, that person will do anything to make you happy. Even if that means making *themselves* unhappy. That person starts to think they know what's best for you and will let their own insecurities get the best of them," she explained. "I've been in situations like that before. It's not easy to fix," she warned.

I breathed out, looking at her. "I just feel so lost. I don't know what to do anymore," I confessed.

My mom ran her fingers through my hair. "Oh, Caleb. You were always such a good kid. You never talked back, never broke the rules, and you always put your heart and soul into everything," she said wistfully. "You always think of others first and put yourself second. This time, you need to put yourself first and think about what *you* need," she advised.

I stared at the carpet. "Yeah, you're right. I just don't know what to do about this whole mess," I said.

"I think you need to ask yourself what you want."

I tried to focus. What *did* I want? I didn't want to hide anymore, that's for sure. I didn't want to lie anymore, either. And also…I wanted *him*.

"I think you should tell your fans the truth. If they are your true fans, they will stay by your side and keep supporting you. You just have to believe that everything will work itself out," my mom said.

I knew she was right; there was no point in lying anymore. I smiled at my mom and hugged her tightly. "Thank you, Mom," I said gratefully.

She rubbed my back as we hugged. "Oh, sweetie. I love you. I hope my words helped."

Just then, my sister came down the stairs.

"Hey," she said, obviously concerned.

I stood up and gave her a hug. "Hi," I replied, squeezing her tightly which I knew she hated. She studied my face.

"Are you ok?" she asked.

I shrugged. "I'm…still here. I'm not completely ok, but I think I will be," I answered.

She nodded slowly. "I was so pissed when I heard. *Fuck* the paparazzi," she said with anger.

My mom looked at her and frowned. "Language!" she warned. "Although, I do agree with you." Sofia and I laughed.

"Thank you, both. I feel a bit better now," I said. Right then, my phone buzzed. I looked and it was a message from my agent. *Oh, what now?* I thought. I opened it and read.

Hi, Caleb. Thought this might cheer you up a bit.

There was an attachment.

Congratulations! You have been nominated for a Golden Globe award as Best Leading Actor in a Dramatic Film. The awards will commence this upcoming Saturday. We look forward to seeing you then!

I gasped, the phone dropping from my hands. My mom stood up immediately, alarmed.

"Oh, no. Is it another leak?" she asked.

I shook my head and tried to get the words out. "I've been nominated for a Golden Globe!" I exclaimed in disbelief.

My mom and sister both gasped at the news. "Oh, honey, congratulations!" my mom yelled.

Sofia looked at me in amazement. "That's awesome."

I hugged them both and for a moment, I forgot about my problems.

"See?" my mom said. "There's always a rainbow after some rain!" she said with a knowing tone. I grinned from ear to ear, still in disbelief. I'd been nominated for awards before, but never for one like the Golden Globes. This was *incredible.* Maybe things would start to look up, after all.

As I pulled up to my apartment, I felt lighter, the adrenaline of the news still rushing through me. The *Golden fucking Globes.* Even if I didn't win, I was still honored to be nominated. I parked my car and got out. It had begun to get dark already and I was about to enter my apartment when I heard footsteps. I turned around cautiously, and I didn't see anything at first through the darkness. Then, a figure emerged from the shadows. My heartbeat quickened and my throat closed. Then light hit the mysterious figure's face and I saw it was...*Brent*? I shook my head in confusion.

"What the hell are *you* doing here?"

He just leaned on my car and smiled smugly. "I was in the neighborhood."

I took a few steps backwards. "What do you want?" I asked, my voice quavering.

Brent looked around casually. "Oh, nothing. I just heard about how everybody knows your little secret now," he said innocently.

Anger pulsed through my veins and my cheeks burned. "What the fuck is your problem?" I said, my voice echoing. "You came here to laugh at my misfortune? That's pathetic, even for you," I spat out.

Brent just laughed mockingly. "It's a shame, though. You really ought to be more careful about what you do in public," he said nastily. There was something else in his voice, though. Something that turned the gears in my brain and I gaped at him, realization dawning on me.

"Did...did *you* take that photo?" I asked in disbelief.

Brent just shrugged. "I'm not confirming nor denying that. I *might* have given the tabloids a little push, though," he said, gloating.

I shook my head, so many emotions coming into me at once. I didn't even know what to *say.* "You're fucking crazy," I finally got out. "This...this isn't some *game.* These are people's *lives* you're fucking with. Don't you understand that?!" I shouted.

Brent smiled, not a care in the world. "I told you, Caleb. That you would regret it." I clenched my fists, wanting to fucking beat the *living shit* out of this dirtbag.

Brent backed away. "Don't even think about touching me. It'll just ruin your reputation even more," he said. Then he backed into the shadows and walked away. Just like that.

I stood there on the driveway, breathing heavily. Tears formed in my eyes. How could someone be so *evil?*

I didn't understand it at all.

CHAPTER 27

Aaron

The next Saturday, I was at home watching *Bleeding Rose* for the hundredth time. I drank from a bottle of tequila while I watched, getting a little buzzed. I stared at Caleb on the screen. He was shirtless in this scene, about to have sex with a girl. Jealousy prickled at me. *Not fucking fair. Get your hands off him. That boy is mine.* I laughed at myself. How pathetic. I was getting jealous over a fictional relationship. I really have hit rock bottom. Since I wasn't seeing Caleb anymore, this was my only way of looking at him. Although, it wasn't the same at all. I couldn't touch him, couldn't smell him. I couldn't kiss him or hold his hand. I sighed and took a swig. *What was my life coming to?* My phone rang, and I glanced at it. It was Tracy. I put the bottle down and answered the call.

"What's up?" I asked apathetically.

"You sound excited. What are you up to?" she asked.

I looked around. "Oh, just watching Caleb have sex with some girl on my TV screen while drinking tequila. Nothing new," I answered nonchalantly.

"…I see," Tracy said, obviously troubled by my response. "Anyway," she said, switching topics. "I have an extra pass to the Golden Globe's today. My friend canceled on me at the last minute. Wanna come?" she asked.

"No," I replied.

A pause. "Why the hell not?" Tracy demanded.

I burped. "I don't want to see Caleb and his blue eyes," I admitted. I had heard Caleb was nominated for an award. I don't think I could handle seeing him right now.

"Ugh, Aaron. I'm just gonna come out and ask: do you regret breaking things off with Caleb?"

I paused. "Well…I didn't want to break things off. I did it because I thought it would be better for him," I explained.

Tracy made a frustrated noise. "Aaron, you idiot. You're obviously depressed and you obviously miss Caleb. You've been saying what you want, but have you thought about what *he* wants?" she asked, expecting an answer.

"I just don't want to weigh him down—"

"Oh, enough with the bullshit. You're letting your own insecurities get in the way of your happiness. I know

I told you this relationship was a bad idea at first, but I can tell that you guys are both disgustingly and totally in love with each other. It's sickening. If you want him back, go and do something about it instead of sulking on your ass!" she shouted.

I was silent. "You're one to talk, you know," I said finally.

Tracy laughed. "I know. That's another thing I wanted to tell you. I'm breaking up with you," she said casually.

I narrowed my eyes. "Uh…what?" I asked.

"You heard me. I'm done with this fake relationship. I don't know when or how, but I'm eventually going to tell the world the truth. I don't want to hide anymore, not when I'm in love. It's not fair to me or to Sasha," she said, a fierceness in her tone.

I was shocked to hear this and didn't quite know what to say. "I'm…I'm happy for you," I finally said. "I think that's pretty brave of you to do."

"Thanks. I think it's your turn now to be brave," Tracy countered.

I rubbed my face, not knowing what to do. "Alright, Tracy. I'll take your advice into consideration," I said.

"So you're not gonna come?" she asked.

"I don't think so," I said apologetically.

Tracy sighed. "Fine. Whatever. At least think about what I said, though," she pleaded. Then we hung up.

I stood up, pausing the television. It coincidentally paused on a close-up shot of Caleb, his blue eyes piercing into me. I stared at him, thinking about what Tracy said. *If you want him back, go and do something about it!* I clenched my fists. It wasn't *that* easy. Then, Megan's words popped into my head.

It's not like you to give up so easily. I breathed out. *Was I giving up easily? Was this better for Caleb, or was I just running away as usual? What about what he wants?* Tracy's words echoed in my head. I stared again at Caleb on the screen, my heart hammering. Memories flashed into my mind. The initial disastrous filming, our dates, his smile, his eyes. The way he saw the *good* in me, even with my flaws. I grabbed my phone, looking to see what time the awards show started.

Oh, shit. It would start at 6 p.m. and it was already 5:35. *Would I even make it on time?* Only one way to find out.

I was driving like a madman, speeding, swerving, and changing lanes. Fuck LA traffic. I was getting a sense of déjà vu, remembering when I rushed to find Caleb at the karaoke bar. I just hoped Caleb wouldn't be too pissed at me. I was such a dumb shit for not realizing sooner. I was the one who was running away, frightened by my own insecurities. I was using Caleb's wellbeing as an excuse for all of that. I almost ran a traffic light when I finally saw the building. I parked haphazardly nearby, almost crashing into the car next to me. I hoped Tracy would be around with that extra pass. I walked around the perimeter aimlessly, but I didn't see her. There were too many people, all dressed up and surrounded by photographers. *God damn it.* I would never find Caleb or Tracy in this crowd.

Security guarded the entrance, so that was out of the question. I looked around for a moment and thought, *ah fuck it.* I sprinted and shoved my way past people, eventually getting to the entrance. Security looked at me in surprise, but I raced right past them and into the building. I could hear them yelling and chasing after me, my heart racing fast. *I'm fucking crazy,* I thought as I ran. I hooked a left, and when they weren't looking, I backed into an empty hallway. I peeked my head out, but I didn't see them anywhere. I saw a sign that pointed to the theater. *There we go.* I ducked into one of the empty aisles of the theater and sat down, breathing heavily. The security team seemed to have lost me for the moment, but I knew they'd spot me eventually. I had to be quick about this. I looked around, trying to find Caleb's face, but I didn't see him. Then, I looked up and... there *he was. Onstage.* He was accepting an award.

Holy fucking shit. *He won.*

CHAPTER 28

Caleb

"And the award for Best Leading Actor in a Drama Film goes to…Caleb Robinson!"

I blinked in surprise, not believing it. I released my long-held breath and saw myself up on the screen. *Did I actually just win a Golden Globe?* My family shouted and clapped, and hugged me all at once. I slowly stood up, my legs like jelly as the audience roared. Somehow my brain told my body to walk, and I carefully went up the stage, shaking hands with the announcer. I took the award in my hands, which was *heavy* by the way. Tears glistened in my eyes. This felt unbelievable. As the cheering died down, I realized I was expected to say something—give a little speech. My heart drummed with anxiety. I didn't even know what to say. Except…that I did. I leaned into the mic and smiled.

"Thank you so much, everyone. This means so much to me, and it is a dream come true. I wanted to thank my family, who are all here right now, for always supporting and encouraging me to never give up on my dreams," I said shakily with nervousness. My family whooped and I grinned at them. I was silent for a moment, gathering my thoughts. Something came over me, and I didn't know what it was. I just knew I didn't want to hide or run away anymore. I cleared my throat. "Recently, there's been some rumors floating around about me." The audience went silent. "At first, I was...ashamed. I didn't want to show the world who I truly was. I was scared that it would reject me. And I know that there will be some people out there who *will* reject me. That's fine; I can accept that now. Because I also realized that there are people out there who love and accept me for who I am." I paused and looked at the audience. "The truth is, yeah, I'm gay. And I was scared to share that piece of me with the world, scared I would lose everything. But I haven't. I'm still standing, and I won't hide anymore. Someone once told me that we're acting all the time; that we're always playing a different role with different people. I suppose that's true; but this time, I just want to be *me.* This same person taught me a lot of things recently. What it means to be brave and what it means to love someone with your heart and soul." I realized I was going on for too long, so I tried to wrap things up. "Love can be a scary thing, but also a wonderful thing. If you just open yourself up to it. Anyways, thank you all for everything. Have a good night, everybody," I said.

There was a long period of stunned silence. And then, someone stood up and started clapping. I looked up and my heart froze. It was... *Aaron.* He was there, beaming at me and clapping wildly. I gasped, not believing what I was seeing. And then my family stood up and started clapping, and soon after that, the entire *audience* followed, clapping wildly. I blushed onstage, and I looked back at Aaron who was gone. I frowned, looking around. Suddenly, I saw him running to me. He closed the distance and kissed me, right there on stage in front of *everybody.* I closed my eyes, reveling in the kiss. He pulled back and smiled at me.

"I'm so proud of you," he said. I smiled back, tears streaming down my cheeks. The audience kept cheering as Aaron kissed me again. Then, he leaned into the mic.

"Hi, everybody. You might know me as that crazy actor who flips out on waiters. I'm just gonna steal this lovely man for a minute, if that's alright with you." Then Aaron grabbed my hand and pulled me backstage. Security was waiting there, and they made a move to grab Aaron.

"That's the intruder," one of them said. I shook my head and stood in front of Aaron, spreading my arms.

"It's alright!" I yelled. I looked at him. "He's with me," I explained. The security team just looked at me for a moment and then finally turned away, deciding it wasn't worth the trouble. I turned back to Aaron, shaking my head in disbelief.

"What are you *doing* here?!" I shouted in amazement.

Aaron ran his fingers through his dark hair. "I've been doing a lot of thinking. And I realized that I can't go on without you. You made me a *better man*. I was drowning in my own insecurities, thinking that I wasn't good enough for you. But you helped me to realize that, although I've made mistakes, it's never too late to try and fix them. I'm so sorry, Caleb. For everything." He grabbed my hand and softly kissed it. "I love you. I love you so fucking much and I don't want to lose you," he said.

I smiled, tears soaking my cheeks. "You haven't," I said. "You haven't lost me. I'm right here. I'll *always* be here. I love you too, Aaron." I embraced him tightly, never wanting to let him go. He wrapped his arms around me, and I cried into his chest, all my emotions coming out at once.

"It's okay," he said, stroking my hair. "I'm right here, sweetheart. I'm never leaving you again," he assured me. I breathed out shakily and looked up at him, into those dark, brooding eyes. I stood on my tip-toes and pressed my lips against his. I was home.

Aaron carried me bridal style into my apartment. I was giggling, and maybe a tad tipsy.

"Put me down!" I yelled, laughing. Aaron walked into my room and threw me on the bed.

"As you wish," he said. He took off his shirt, revealing his muscular physique. "I've been waiting for this a long time. I'm all pent up," he said breathlessly. My cock was already beginning to get hard.

"I'm gonna fuck you all night long," Aaron promised. I grinned and took of my shirt, throwing it on the floor. Then I unzipped my pants, throwing those to the floor too. I was just in my pink briefs now and Aaron was looking at me, desire in his eyes.

"Touch yourself," he commanded. My cock twitched at this request and I slowly lowered my briefs, revealing my fully hard penis. I grasped my dick with my right hand and started stroking. I groaned, enjoying the pleasure.

"Fuck," Aaron breathed. "You're so fucking sexy," he said, palming himself through his underwear. "I want you to finger yourself now," he ordered. I nodded and began rubbing my hole, opening myself up gently. I inserted one finger and moaned. *Fuck*. I stroked myself as I inserted another finger, and I threw my head back. Aaron got closer, watching me pleasure myself.

"Yes, that's it. So fucking beautiful," he said, now openly stroking his cock. I spread my legs and inserted a third finger, groaning at the intrusion. Aaron smirked. "Look at you, all spread out with your fingers in your ass. You're like a bitch in heat," he remarked.

This comment made my cock harder, if that was even possible. Aaron got on the bed with me and started fondling my nipples, sucking and biting at them until they were red and perky. I was making little gasping noises, and Aaron grabbed our cocks and started rubbing them together, starting at a slow pace. Oh fuck, it felt *so* good. He picked up the pace and I kept finger-fucking myself. He stopped rubbing them together and looked at me, seemingly possessed.

"Suck my dick," he said, as if there were no option. I nodded, removing my fingers from my hole and leveling myself with his hard cock and grasping at his big balls. I played and sucked at his nutsack, rubbing them against my tongue, swirling them around in my mouth. Then I started stroking his cock, and I bent down to lick the tip. Aaron shuddered and I wrapped my lips around the head, licking up his dripping pre-cum. I started bouncing my head up and down, going deeper which each movement.

"Fuck, yeah," Aaron growled. "You look so pretty with my dick in your mouth," he moaned. Encouraged by this, I started sucking at a faster pace, trying to deepthroat his cock. I could feel the head pop into my throat and I held it there, trying not to gag. "Oh, shit!"

Aaron yelled as I deepthroated him. I released his dick from my mouth, saliva dripping onto the bed, gasping for air. Aaron pushed me down onto the bed.

"I hope your ass is ready to get drilled," he said. "Get on your hands and knees," he demanded, no room for negotiation. I quickly got into position, arching my back so my ass was in the air. I could feel Aaron smack his cock against my ass a couple times and he pressed soft kisses to my back, down to my ass.

"I was thinking…do you want to go bareback?" he asked. I nodded, cock jerking up.

Fuck yes, I wanted that. "I'm negative," I told him.

He nodded. "So am I," he confirmed. He spread my ass cheeks and spat into my hole, rubbing it with his finger. "Gonna cream you up," he grunted as he pushed the head of his cock into my tight pink hole. I yelped as his cock stretched me out, filling me to the brim. It felt like I was being split in half, but the pain felt fucking good. I pushed back against Aaron's dick, and he was fully inside me.

"You alright?" Aaron asked.

I nodded. "Fuck me already!" I shouted, unable to take it anymore. Aaron grinned and stuck his tongue out playfully, and then slammed back into me. He pulled out halfway and rocked into me, fucking me relentlessly.

"Oh, shit!" I yelled as he pounded my ass. He pushed my head down into the bed and fucked me like this, thrusting in and out. I bit the bedsheets and took the pounding, reveling in it. My cock was leaking rivers of pre-cum onto the bed.

"Fucking take this dick!" Aaron shouted as he pulled my hair back and hooked his fingers into my mouth. I whimpered and moaned, licking his fingers. He then shifted and planted his foot onto my head as he fucked me, and *god* it felt surreal. Then Aaron pulled out and told me to get on my back. I did as I was told, and Aaron crashed down on me, kissing me hard. Our tongues were wrapping into each other, and he guided his cock into my ass as we made out. He pushed in and I gasped into his mouth. He started fucking me, and I wrapped my legs around his broad back. He sucked on my neck, and then kissed me again on the mouth, riding into me.

"I love you so fucking much, baby," he said. I nodded, tears forming in my eyes. But these weren't sad tears, these were *happy* tears.

"I love you too!" I shouted as he fucked me mercilessly.

"I'm close, I'm gonna fill you with my cum," Aaron promised. I nodded quickly, and held onto him, my face buried in his hairy, sweaty chest. I could feel him thrust more rapidly and I knew it was coming.

"OH FUCK!" he screamed and I could feel his seed spill into me, splattering my insides. Aaron thrusted into me a little more, before slowly stopping. He collapsed onto me, and we both lay there, panting heavily. After a moment, he slowly lifted his head up and kissed my bottom lip, sucking on it. Then, he slowly began to pull out, and I could feel his cum gushing out my ass, dripping down onto the bed. He stared at my wet hole, admiring it.

"Fuck. I bred you well," he observed. I laughed and beckoned him to lie with me. He lay down and I buried my face into his armpit, my ass throbbing. "How was it? You alright?" Aaron asked. I nodded and looked up at him.

"It was…I can't even put it into words how amazing it was," I confessed. Aaron grinned, sweat dripping down his forehead. He kissed my temple and snuggled into me.

"I never thought I'd fall in love," Aaron admitted after a moment.

I breathed out. "Me either," I said truthfully.

He looked down at me. "I'm glad I met you," he said, his eyes glittering.

I smiled. "I'm glad I met you, too," I replied, *meaning* it. Aaron stroked my hair, and I enveloped myself into his chest. *This was bliss*, I thought as sleep started to overtake me, and I gently closed my eyes as I listened to Aaron's heartbeat.

I had found my *person*, my home. And I would make sure to cherish it, *always*.

EPILOGUE

Aaron

Six Months Later

"How do I look?" Caleb asked, turning from the mirror. I looked up and I looked him up and down. He was wearing a blue button-down shirt with a dark dress jacket, a tie, and slacks. His blond hair was coiffed up with gel. I grinned.

"Like a handsome son of a bitch," I answered. I looked at my reflection and stood next to Caleb. I was wearing a black button-down shirt with a leather jacket, black jeans, and I gelled my long, black hair back. I was also wearing my turtle necklace under my shirt for good luck. Caleb looked at me and smiled.

"You look absolutely sexy," he remarked. I ran a hand through my hair and winked at my reflection.

"You think so?" I asked playfully. He swatted my arm, and I hugged him from the side. I stared at Caleb in the mirror. I still couldn't believe this man was my boyfriend. I looked around at Caleb's room—*our* room,

I corrected myself. I still had to break that habit. Not long after we reconciled, Caleb had invited me to move in with him.

"Are you sure?" I had asked him back then.

"Of course. I want to live with you, and I would love to spend every day waking up next to you," he had replied. I remember I had felt so happy.

"Alright. Let's do it!" I answered. Flash forward to six months later, and we were officially living together. And it was *bliss* waking up every day next to Caleb. I hated waking up in my old house; it was way too big for me, and I felt lonely in it. I gave the property back to my parents, who were shocked and unsurprisingly upset that I had a boyfriend. Just another disappointment to add to the list. I didn't care though. *Caleb* was what mattered to me. He put his hand on my shoulder.

"Are you ready?" he asked. I took another glance at my reflection and breathed out.

"Yeah. I'm ready," I answered. We were heading to Caleb's parents' house for a party to celebrate the premiere of *The Leading Man.* We resumed filming not long after the awards ceremony, and it was a blast to film. Every day on set was an adventure, and it was amazing getting to work with my own boyfriend. The movie was predicted to be a blockbuster hit and was apparently the most anticipated film of the year. I didn't care if it flopped though; I was proud of it either way.

And I know Caleb felt the same. I straightened Caleb's tie and we hit the road in my red mustang. I draped my wrist over the steering wheel, holding Caleb's hand with my other hand. I pulled up to Caleb's parents' house and we knocked on the door. His mother opened the door, wearing a lavender dress. She brightened when she saw us.

"The stars are here!" she yelled and invited us in. I had met Caleb's family before. They were super nice, but I still wasn't used to their kindness and hospitality. After all, I had never shared that kind of warmth with my own family.

"Hi, Aaron," Mrs. Robinson said, giving me a big hug. "It's so good to see you again!" she exclaimed.

"Likewise," I said, hugging her back. Mittens stood on her hind legs and leapt at me. I smiled and patted her small head. I said hello to Caleb's siblings, Sofia and Wes.

"Dude, I heard about you punching that asshole. You're fucking awesome!" Wes said to me. Sofia nodded in agreement. I winced, not wanting to recall that memory. Caleb had told me that his former costar, Brent, was the one who leaked the photo. My response, of course, was to promptly deck him in the jaw. Luckily, he didn't press charges, but I still felt bad about it. Although, according to Caleb, it was "kind of hot in a bad-boy way," which made me laugh. Still, I was trying to learn how to control my anger. I wanted to be a better man, especially now that I was with Caleb. I shook hands with Mr. Robinson, and I said hi to Caleb's friend, Lucy. I went to the beverages, choosing just water. I was trying to not drink as much nowadays. I was trying to cut smoking out too. I looked over at Caleb, who was chatting with Lucy. I smiled; I was glad to be a part of this family now. His mom waltzed up to me.

"So, Aaron. I heard that you're going to school now. Is that true?" she asked in wonderment. I grinned and nodded.

"Shocker, I know," I said. That was another new development. After our movie, I decided to retire from acting and from Hollywood. I decided get my English degree and teaching credentials. It was all thanks to Caleb, who encouraged me to follow my passions. As for Caleb, he was still acting. He was branching out into other roles, different projects. He's straying from romance movies now, trying out different genres like action and horror. I was so proud of him, and I made sure to always tell him that. Caleb walked over to me, grabbing my hand.

"Come outside with me?" he asked. I nodded and we walked out to the backyard, just us two.

"What's up?" I asked. Caleb shrugged and hugged me.

"Nothing. I just wanted to be alone with you for a moment, that's all," he admitted. I laughed and hugged Caleb tightly, resting my chin on his head.

"Your wish is my command," I said. He looked up at me, his eyes sparkling.

"I love you," he said. "You know that, right?" I smiled and nodded.

"I know. I love you too, Caleb. So much," I said, playfully flicking his nose. He blushed and then looked down.

"I... I hope we can be together for a long time," he said nervously. I tilted his chin up, so he was looking at me.

"I'm never leaving your side," I firmly promised. "Not if I have anything to say about it." He beamed and lifted onto his toes. I closed my eyes, and I leaned in, our lips softly touching. The sun began to set behind us, casting a rainbow of colors everywhere.

Thank you, Caleb, I thought to myself.
You are my co-star, my friend, my lover, my everything.
You are my leading man.

THE END.

ACKNOWLEDGMENTS

Wow! I cannot believe I am publishing a second book! Publishing books has always been a dream of mine and I am so happy to share my art with you and the world. As a gay man, I am constantly looking for queer love stories in stores like Barnes and Noble. I am honored to add to that section of LGBTQ romance. Our love is no different, and our stories also deserve to be told! I am grateful to put this love out into the world. I hope that others can see that our love is just that: love!

There are many people who I must thank for making this book possible.

To my mom and dad (Charlotte and Asif) for supporting my art and always encouraging me to create and share my art with the world. I would never be able to have the confidence to share my art without your support. Thank you both for making this dream come true! I love you both dearly!

To my brother and sister (Westley and Lyric) for being the best siblings. You guys are very supportive of me and never fail to keep encouraging me. I will always be there for you guys, and I know you both will always be there for me. I love you guys!

To my best friend, Kai, for always supporting and believing in me. You always tell me that I can do it, and you always have had faith in me to do whatever I set my mind to. For this I am extremely grateful. I know you've got my back and I always have yours. Love you!

To my late grandmother, Mangas, for always accepting me. I miss you so much and I wish you were here to see this accomplishment, but I know you are watching from Heaven. I love you so much!

To my editor, Thea, for editing my second book. Just like the first, you did a great job and I'm so thankful for your hard work.

To May, for designing the cover art. I absolutely am in love with the cover and you did a great job bringing Caleb and Aaron to life! It's exactly what I imagined in my head! You're so talented and I can't wait to work with you again!

To Paul, for the beautiful formatting of this book. You make it look so professional and I'm thankful for your work!

And finally, thank you, the reader! Thank you for joining me on this journey and I hope Aaron and Caleb's story empowered you in some way. I hope they taught you something about love, and how fragile but beautiful it is. Thank you for giving this story a chance!

ABOUT THE AUTHOR

Noah Khan was born in Los Angeles and raised in Orange, California. Just like Caleb, he dreams of becoming an actor. He writes songs and records music as a hobby and released his first EP on Spotify. He's also an avid collector of dolls and stuffed animals and is a huge queer romance reader. He has three pets: two dogs and a parrot. *The Leading Man* is his second published work.